THE FIRST-DATE DILEMMA

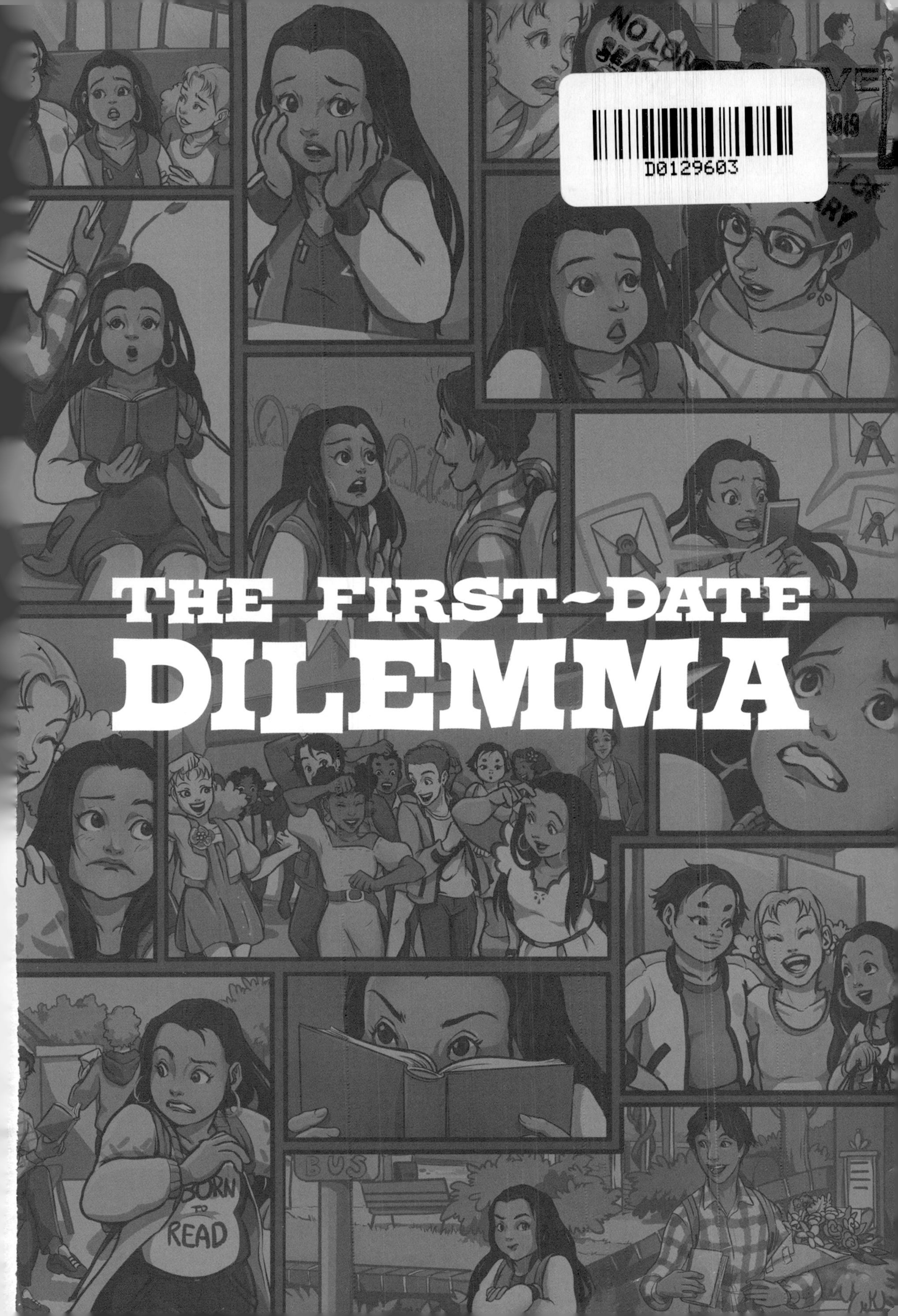
BORN TO READ
BUS

JUNIOR HIGH DRAMA IS PUBLISHED BY
STONE ARCH BOOKS
A CAPSTONE IMPRINT
1710 ROE CREST DRIVE
NORTH MANKATO, MINNESOTA 56003
WWW.MYCAPSTONE.COM

Summary: The eighth graders at Memorial Middle School are obsessing about their first boy-girl party. Lucia is sick of hearing people talk about what to wear and who's going together. If her best friend hadn't insisted, she wouldn't even be going to the dumb party. But after she gets to know Adesh, Lucia starts thinking the party might not be too bad ... until she realizes he's interested in another girl.

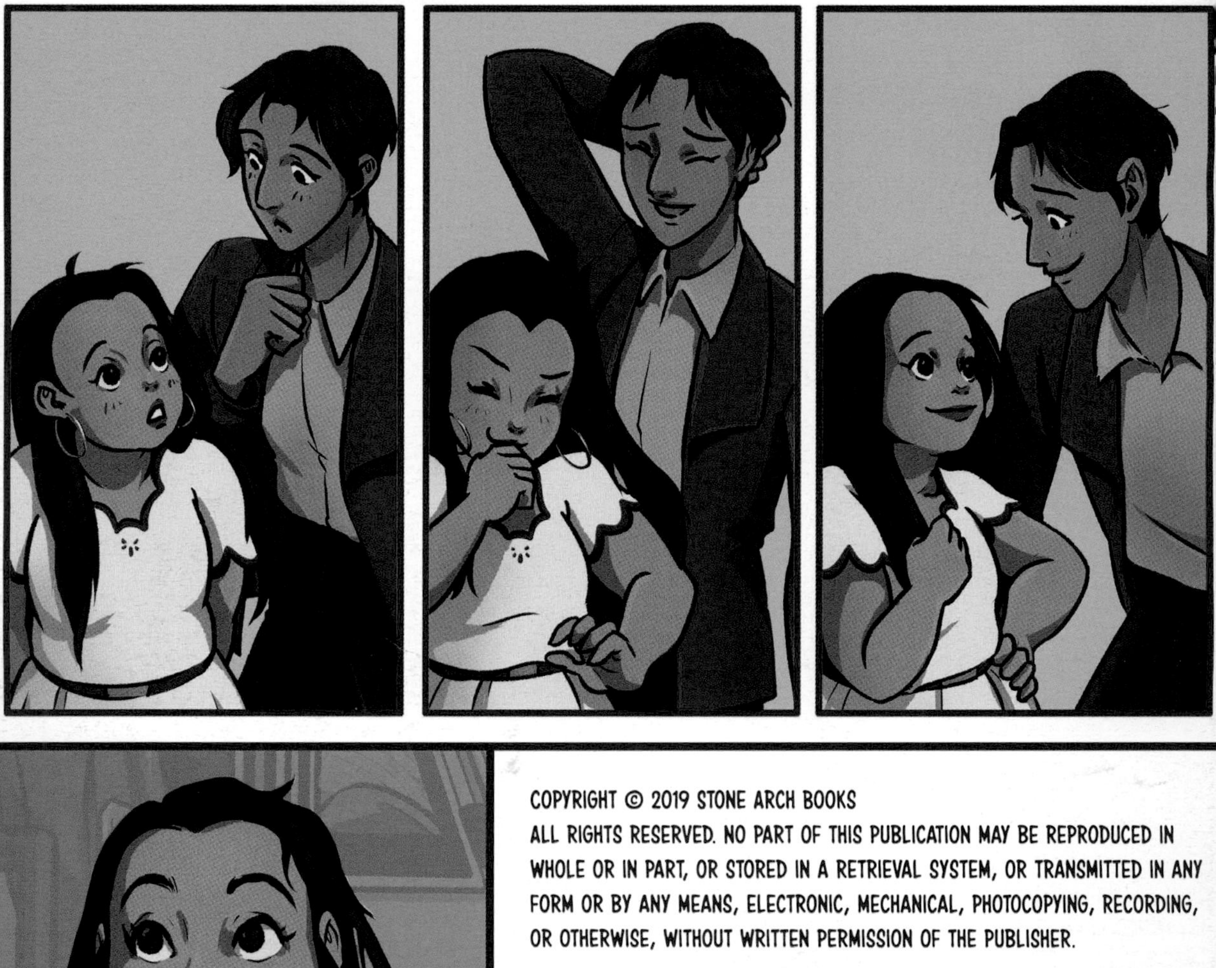

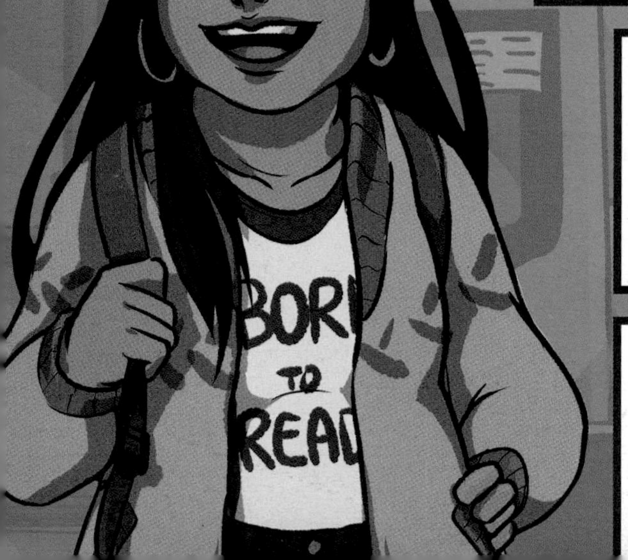

CATALOGING-IN-PUBLICATION DATA IS AVAILABLE ON THE LIBRARY OF CONGRESS WEBSITE.
ISBN: 978-1-4965-4709-5 (LIBRARY BINDING)
ISBN: 978-1-4965-7411-4 (PAPERBACK)
ISBN: 978-1-4965-4714-9 (EBOOK PDF)

EDITOR: JULIE GASSMAN
DESIGNER: ASHLEE SUKER
CREATIVE DIRECTOR: NATHAN GASSMAN

Printed in the United States of America.
PA017

JUNIOR HIGH DRAMA

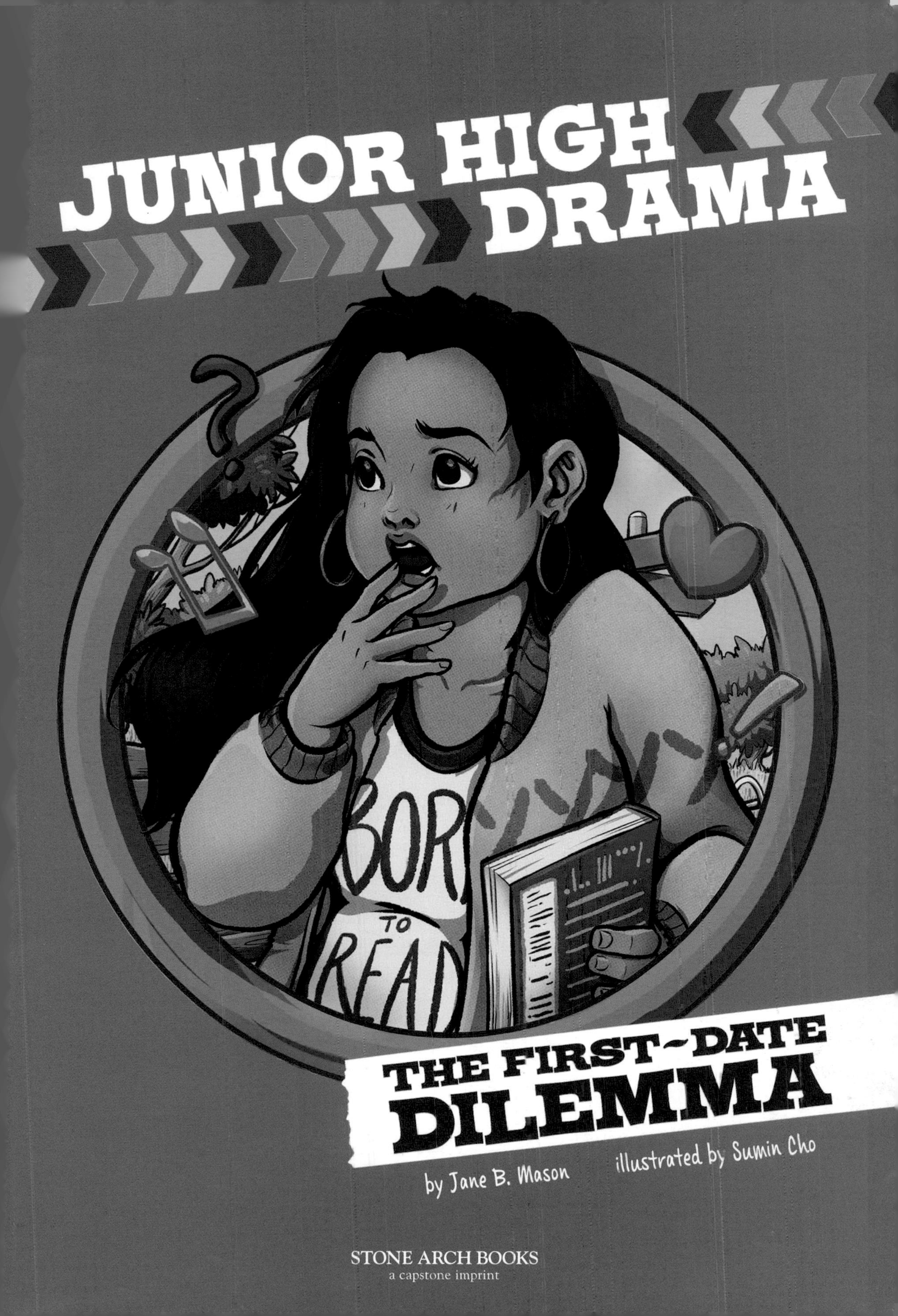

THE FIRST-DATE DILEMMA

by Jane B. Mason
illustrated by Sumin Cho

STONE ARCH BOOKS
a capstone imprint

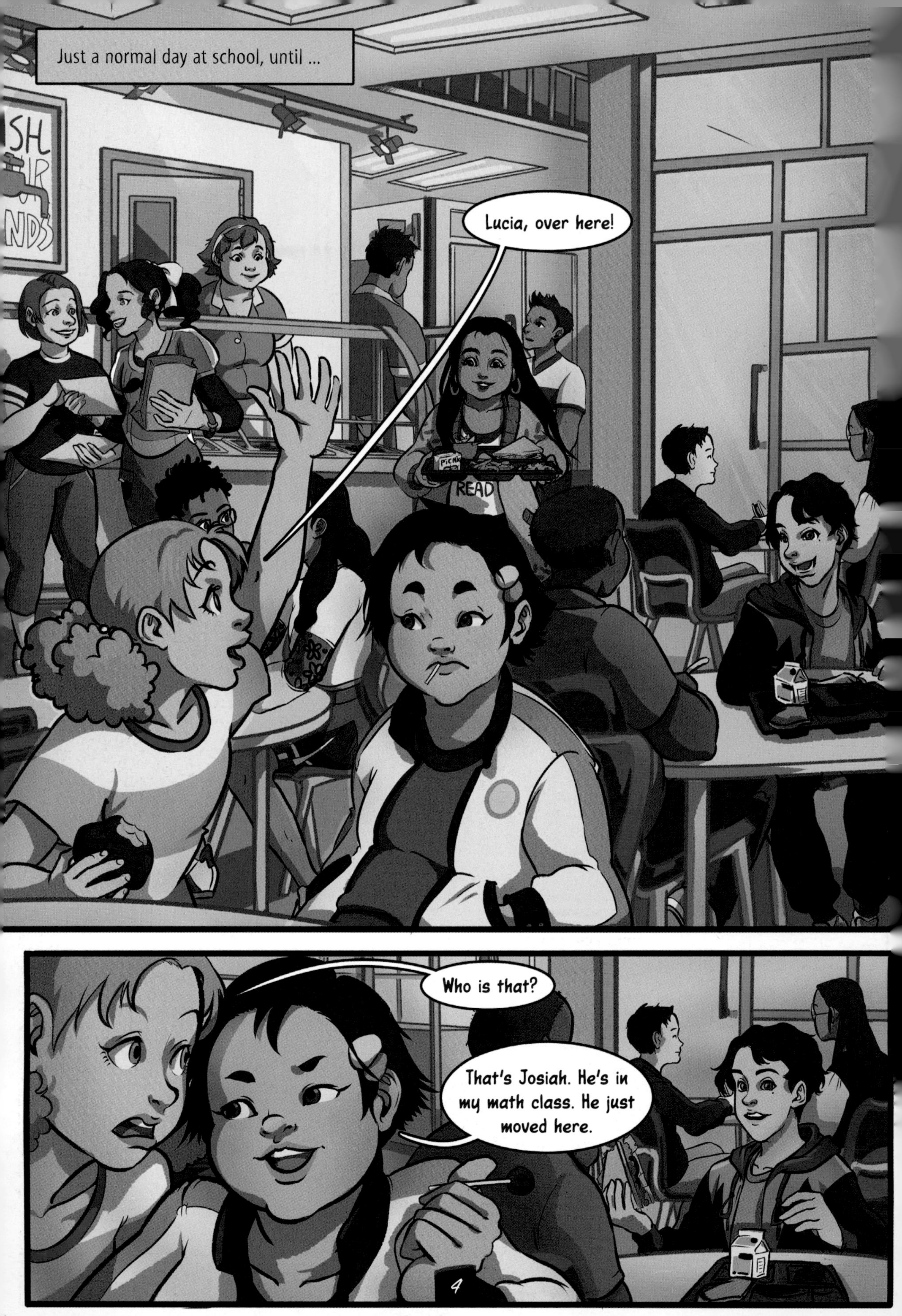
Just a normal day at school, until ...
Lucia, over here!
READ
Who is that?
That's Josiah. He's in my math class. He just moved here.

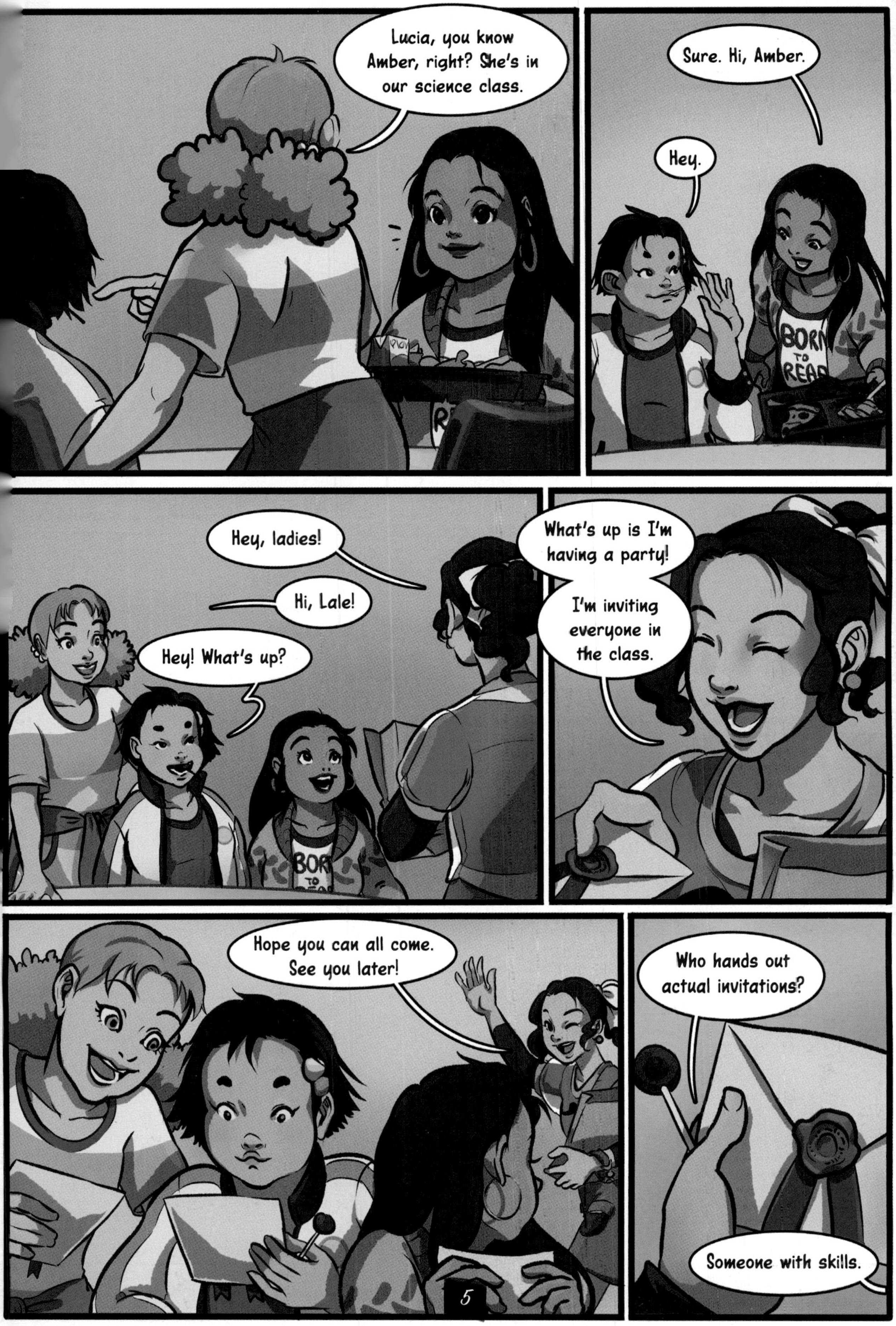
Lucia, you know Amber, right? She's in our science class.
Sure. Hi, Amber.
Hey.
Hey, ladies!
Hi, Lale!
Hey! What's up?
What's up is I'm having a party!
I'm inviting everyone in the class.
Hope you can all come. See you later!
Who hands out actual invitations?
Someone with skills.

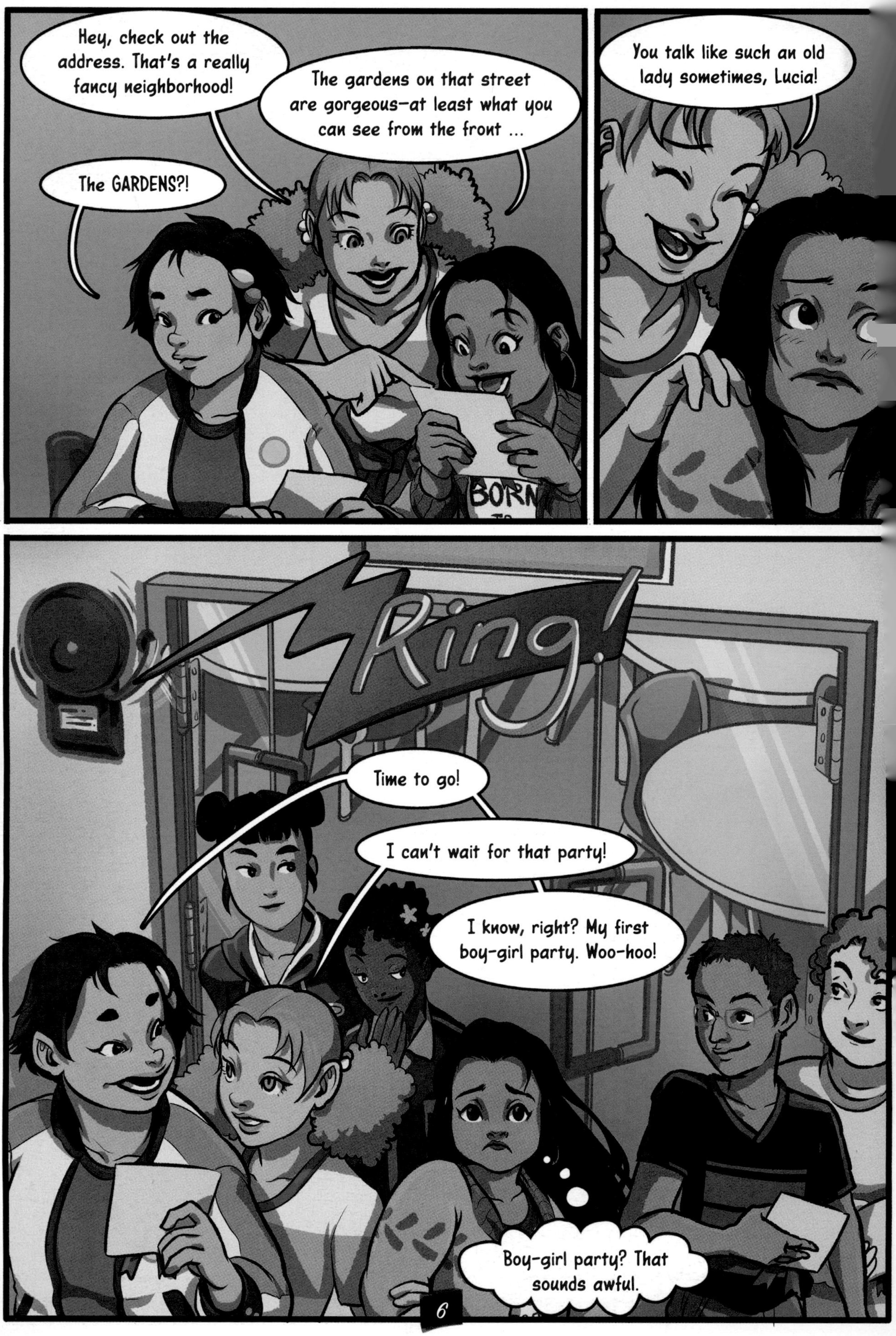

Hey, check out the address. That's a really fancy neighborhood!
The gardens on that street are gorgeous–at least what you can see from the front ...
The GARDENS?!
BORN
You talk like such an old lady sometimes, Lucia!
Ring!
Time to go!
I can't wait for that party!
I know, right? My first boy-girl party. Woo-hoo!
Boy-girl party? That sounds awful.

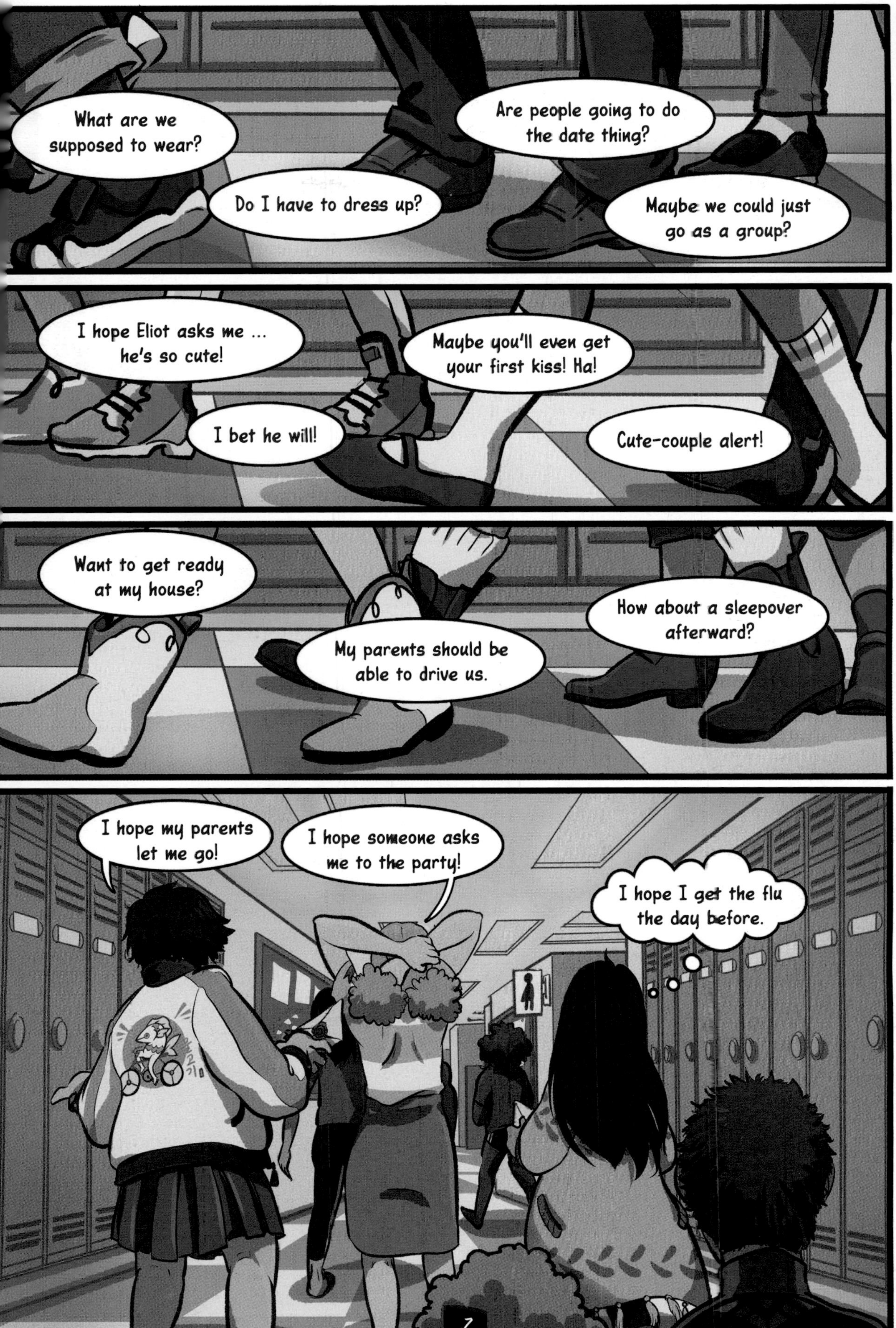
What are we supposed to wear?
Are people going to do the date thing?
Do I have to dress up?
Maybe we could just go as a group?
I hope Eliot asks me ... he's so cute!
Maybe you'll even get your first kiss! Ha!
I bet he will!
Cute-couple alert!
Want to get ready at my house?
How about a sleepover afterward?
My parents should be able to drive us.
I hope my parents let me go!
I hope someone asks me to the party!
I hope I get the flu the day before.

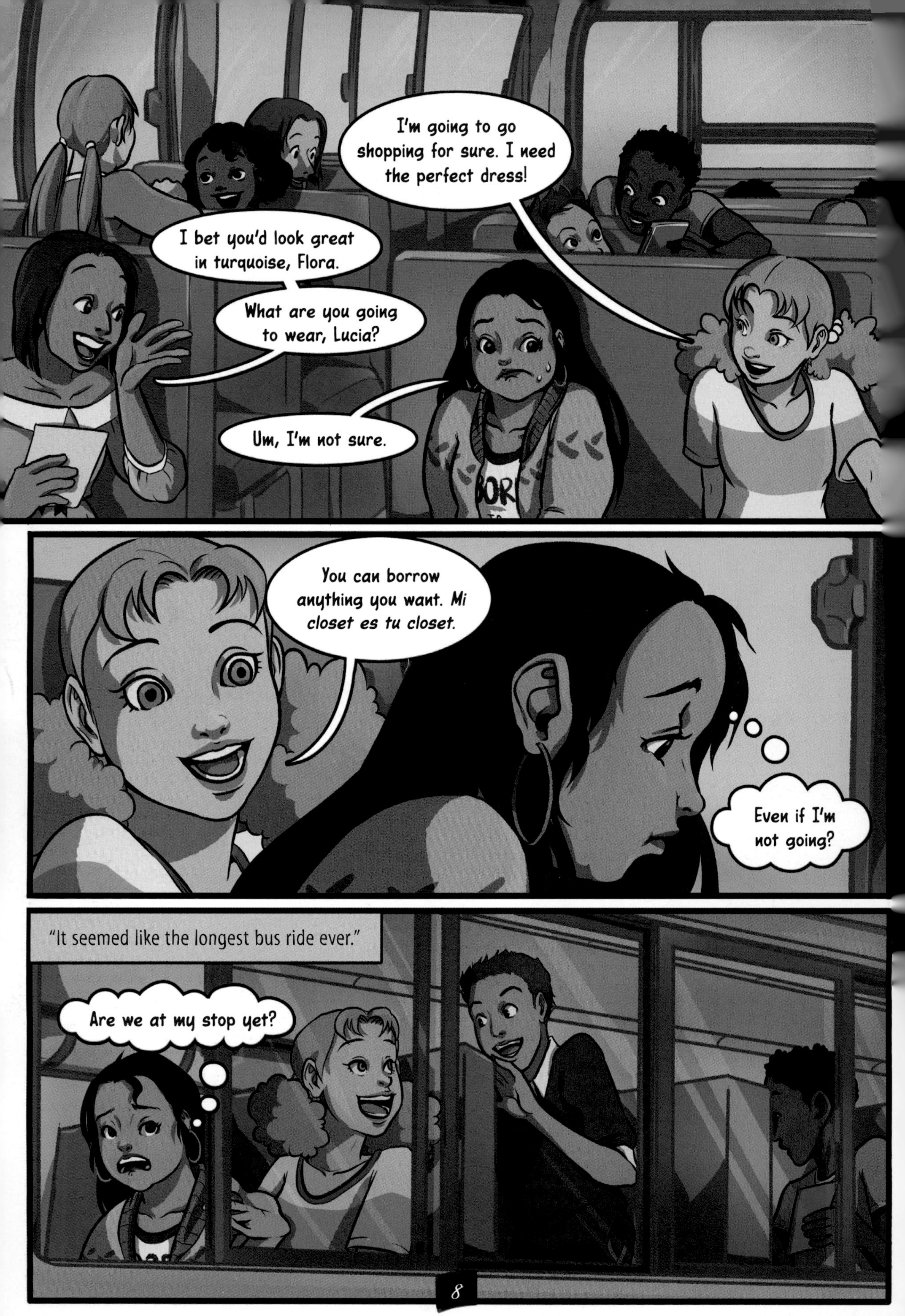
I'm going to go shopping for sure. I need the perfect dress!
I bet you'd look great in turquoise, Flora.
What are you going to wear, Lucia?
Um, I'm not sure.
You can borrow anything you want. *Mi closet es tu closet.*
Even if I'm not going?
"It seemed like the longest bus ride ever."
Are we at my stop yet?

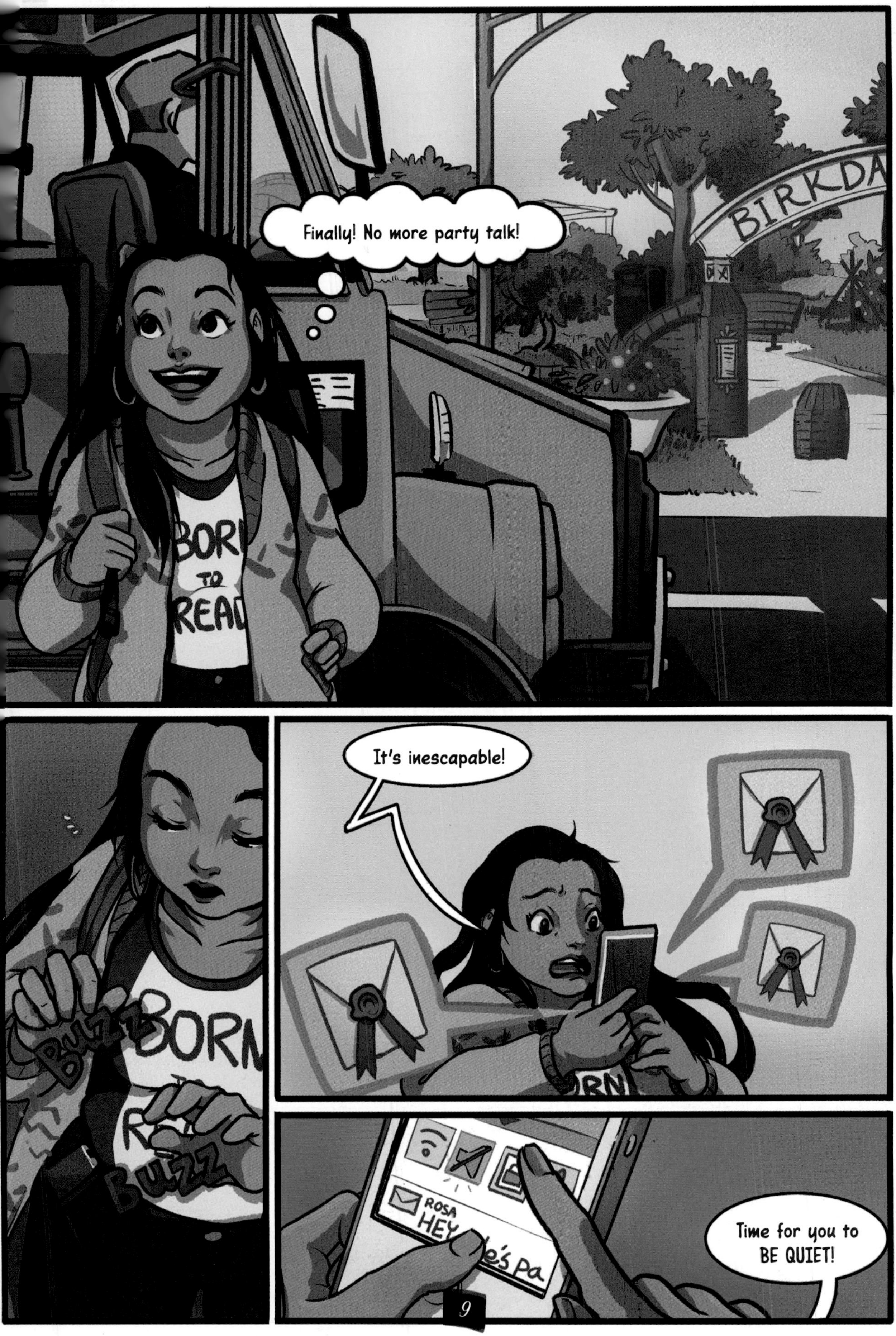

BIRKDA
Finally! No more party talk!
BORN TO READ
BUZZ
BUZZ
It's inescapable!
ROSA
HEY
Time for you to BE QUIET!

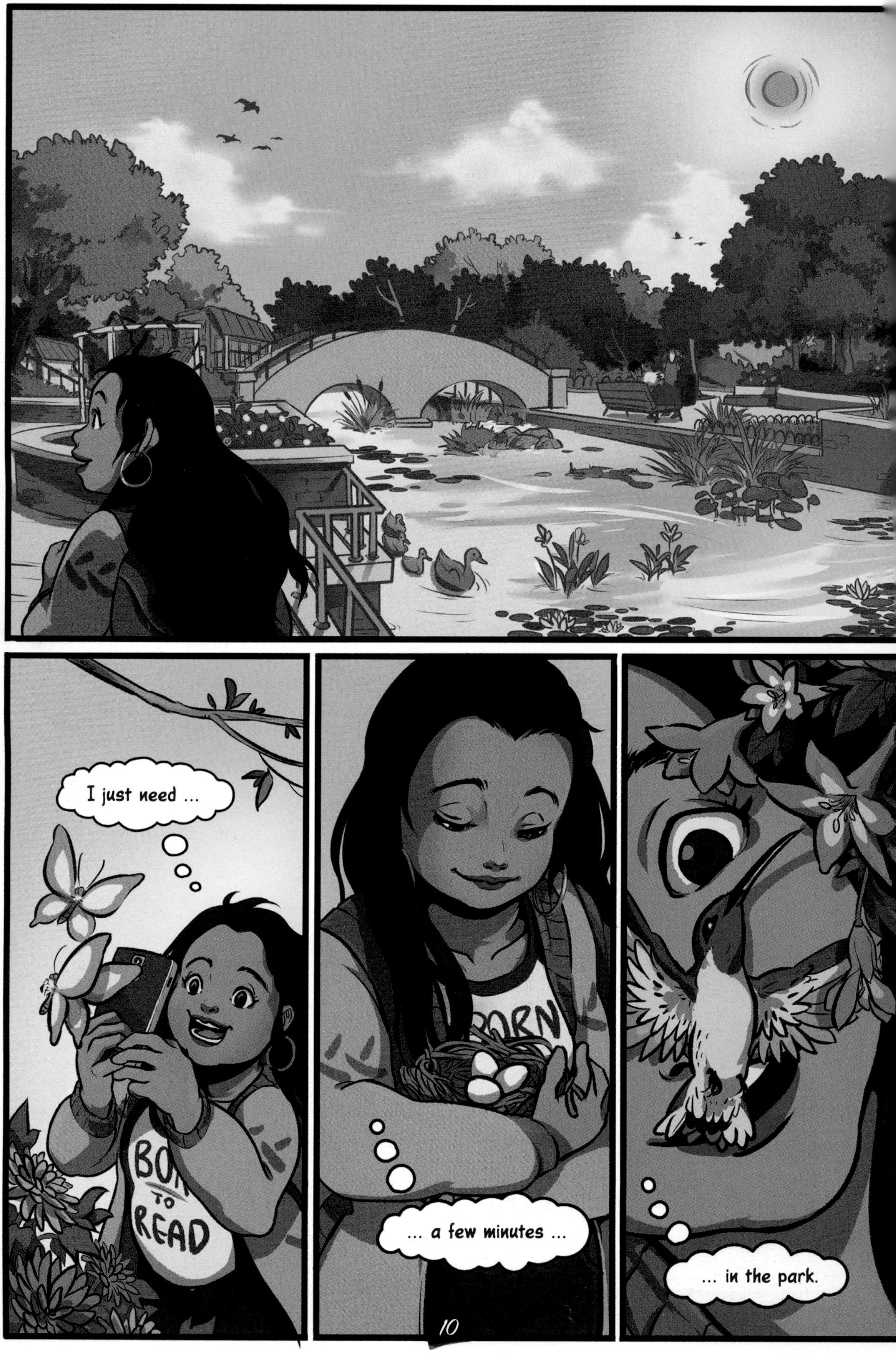
I just need ...
BORN TO READ
... a few minutes ...
... in the park.

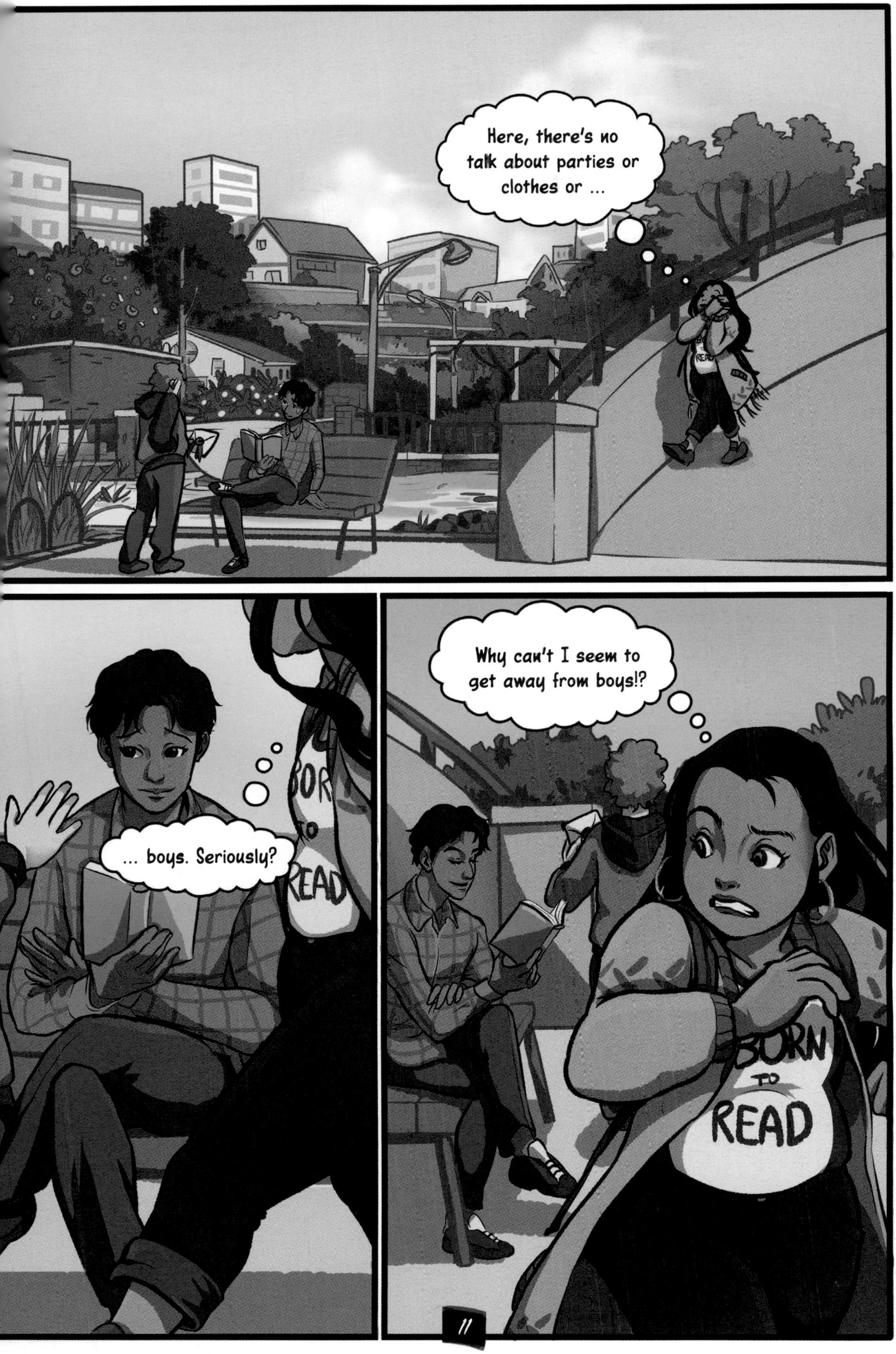
Here, there's no talk about parties or clothes or ...
READ
BORN TO READ
... boys. Seriously?
Why can't I seem to get away from boys!?
BORN TO READ

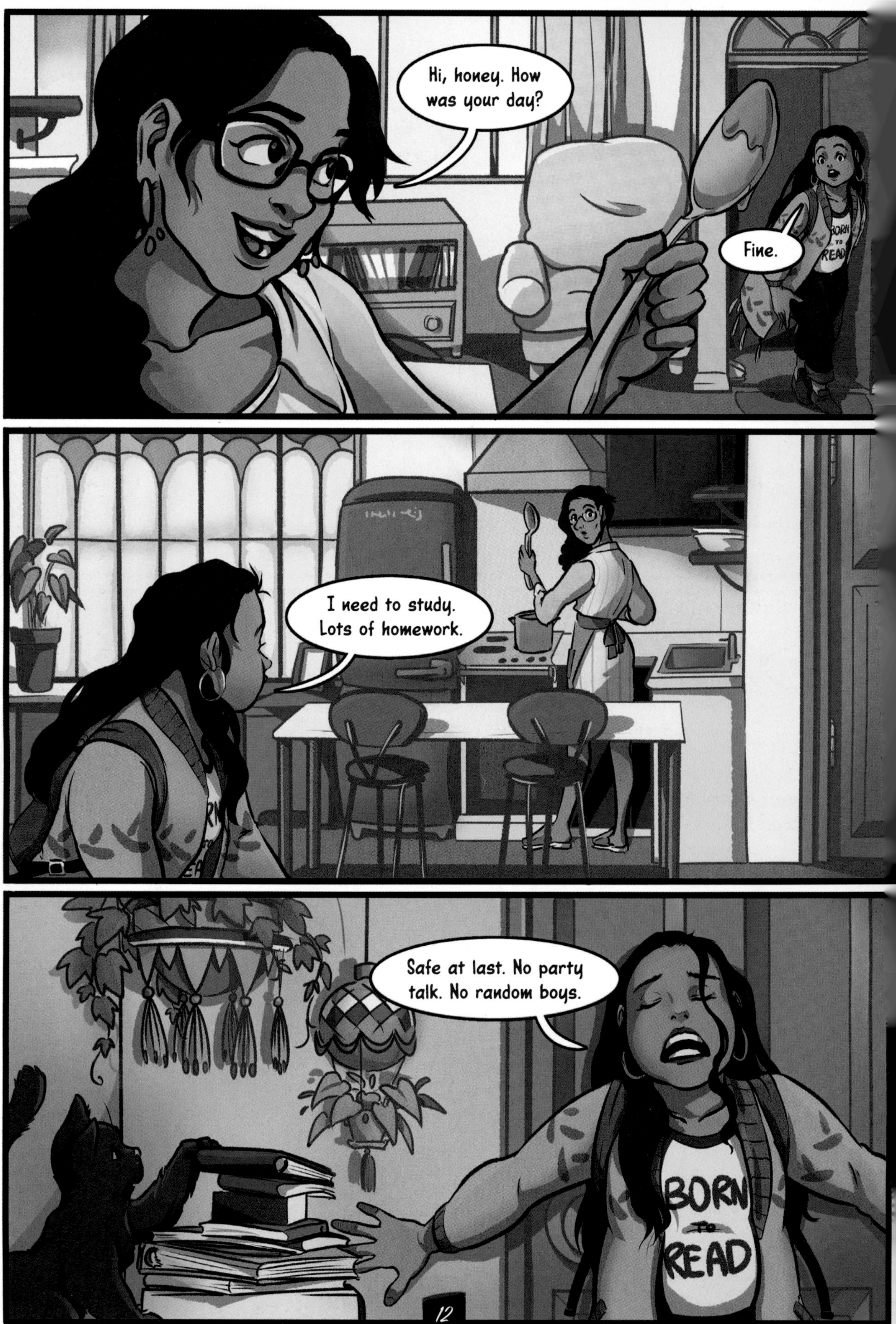
Hi, honey. How was your day?
Fine.
BORN TO READ
I need to study. Lots of homework.
Safe at last. No party talk. No random boys.
BORN TO READ

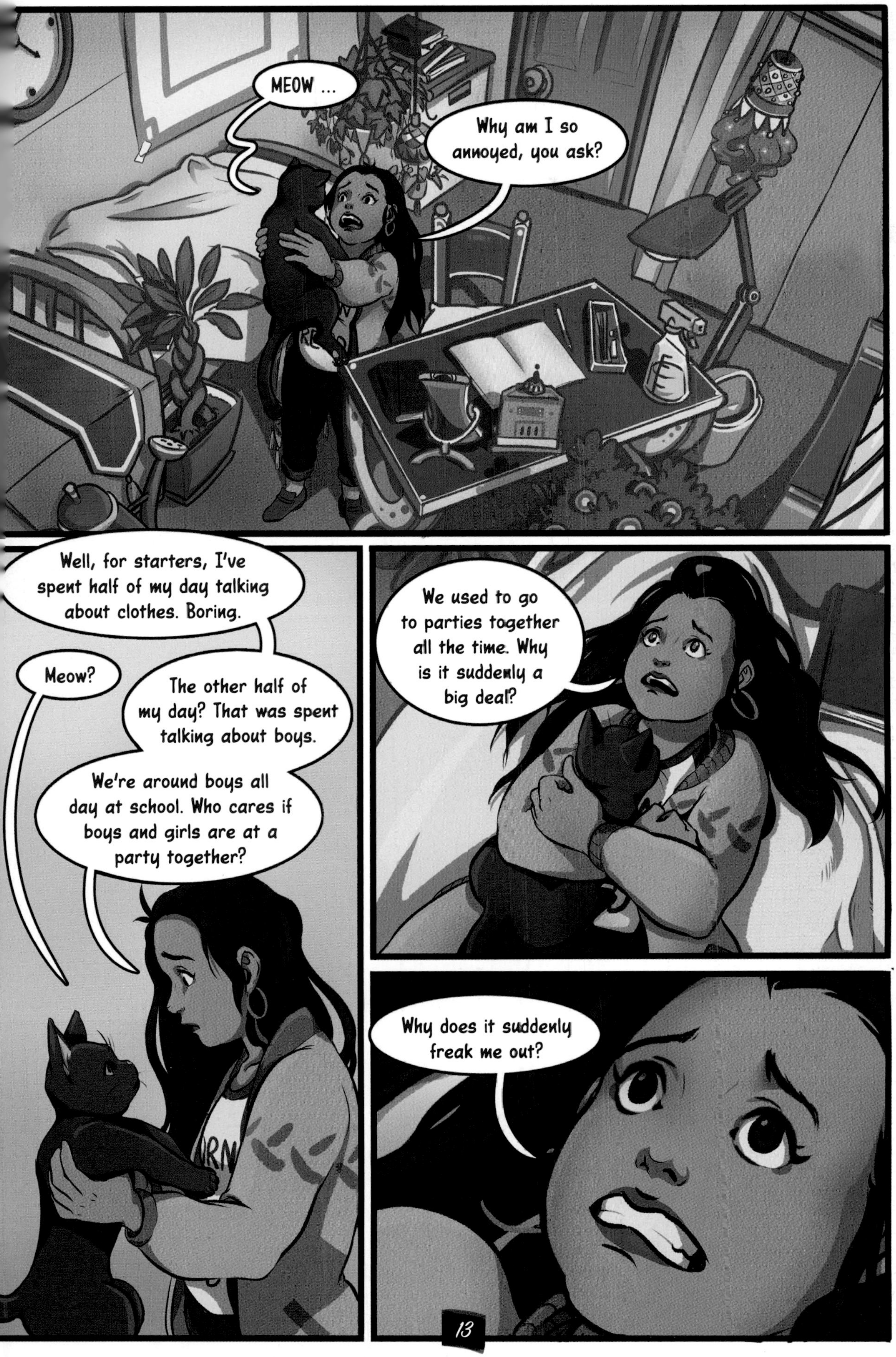
MEOW ...
Why am I so annoyed, you ask?
Well, for starters, I've spent half of my day talking about clothes. Boring.
Meow?
The other half of my day? That was spent talking about boys.
We're around boys all day at school. Who cares if boys and girls are at a party together?
We used to go to parties together all the time. Why is it suddenly a big deal?
Why does it suddenly freak me out?

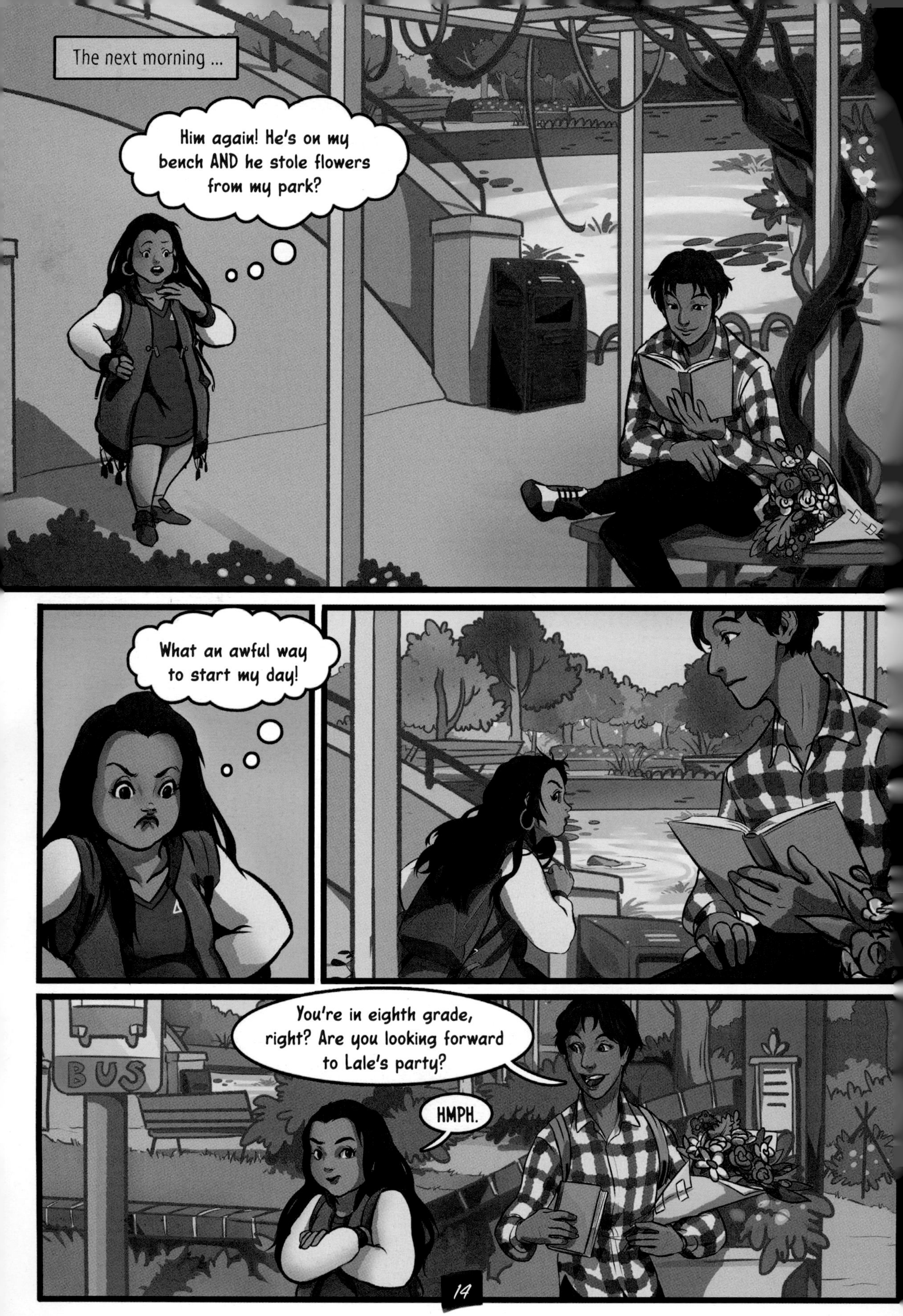
The next morning ...
Him again! He's on my bench AND he stole flowers from my park?
What an awful way to start my day!
You're in eighth grade, right? Are you looking forward to Lale's party?
HMPH.
BUS

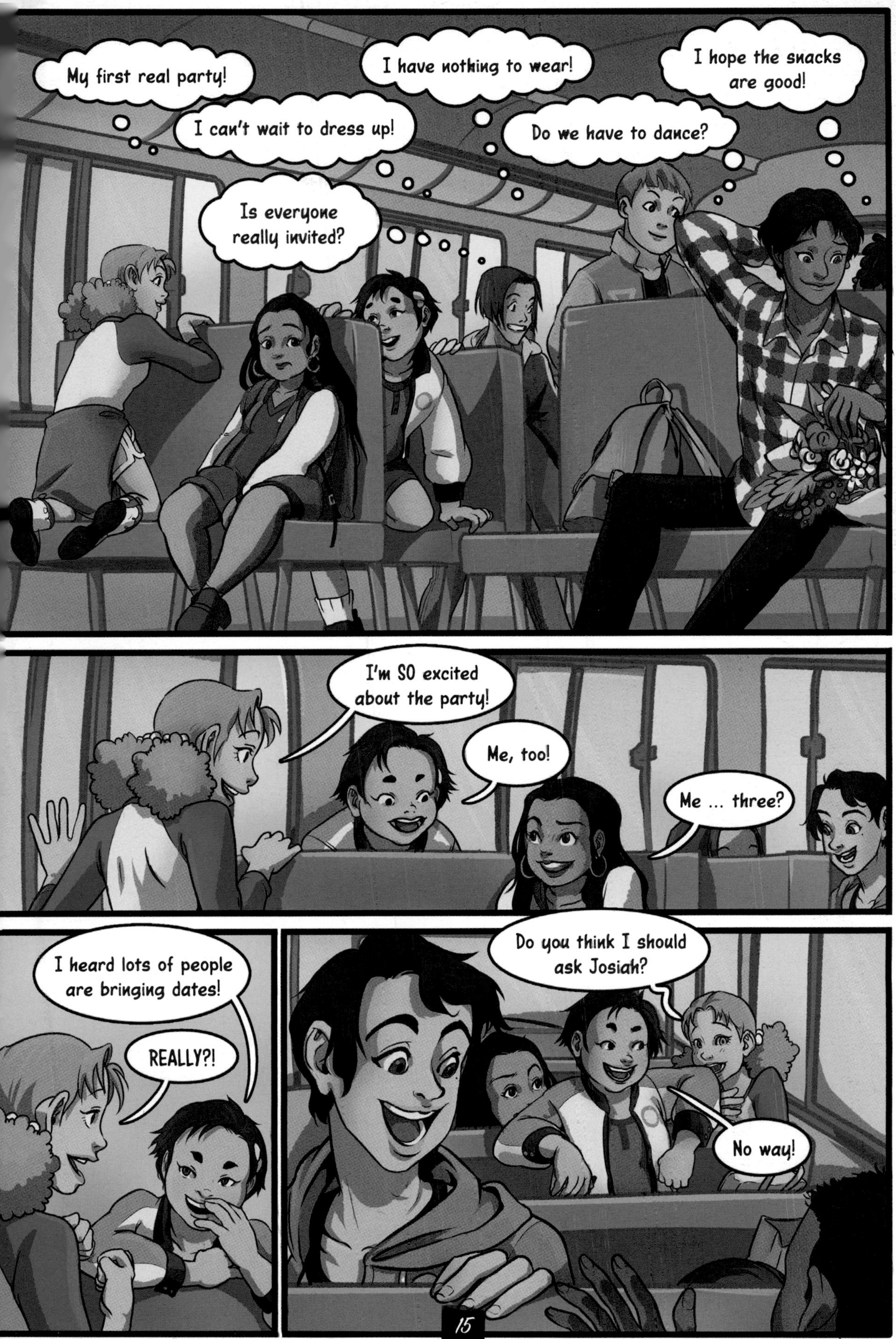
My first real party!
I can't wait to dress up!
Is everyone really invited?
I have nothing to wear!
Do we have to dance?
I hope the snacks are good!
I'm SO excited about the party!
Me, too!
Me ... three?
I heard lots of people are bringing dates!
REALLY?!
Do you think I should ask Josiah?
No way!

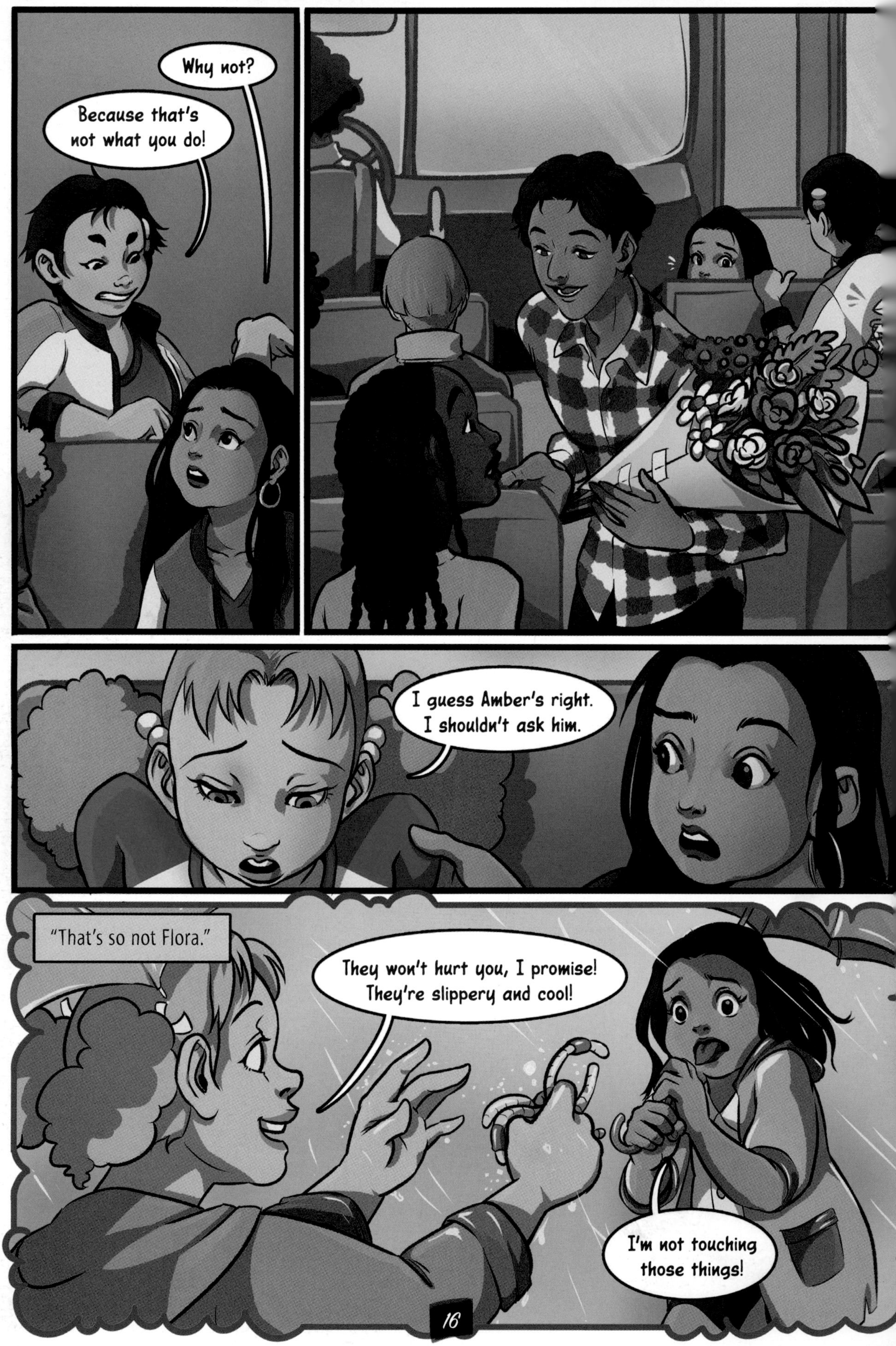

Why not?
Because that's not what you do!
I guess Amber's right. I shouldn't ask him.
"That's so not Flora."
They won't hurt you, I promise! They're slippery and cool!
I'm not touching those things!

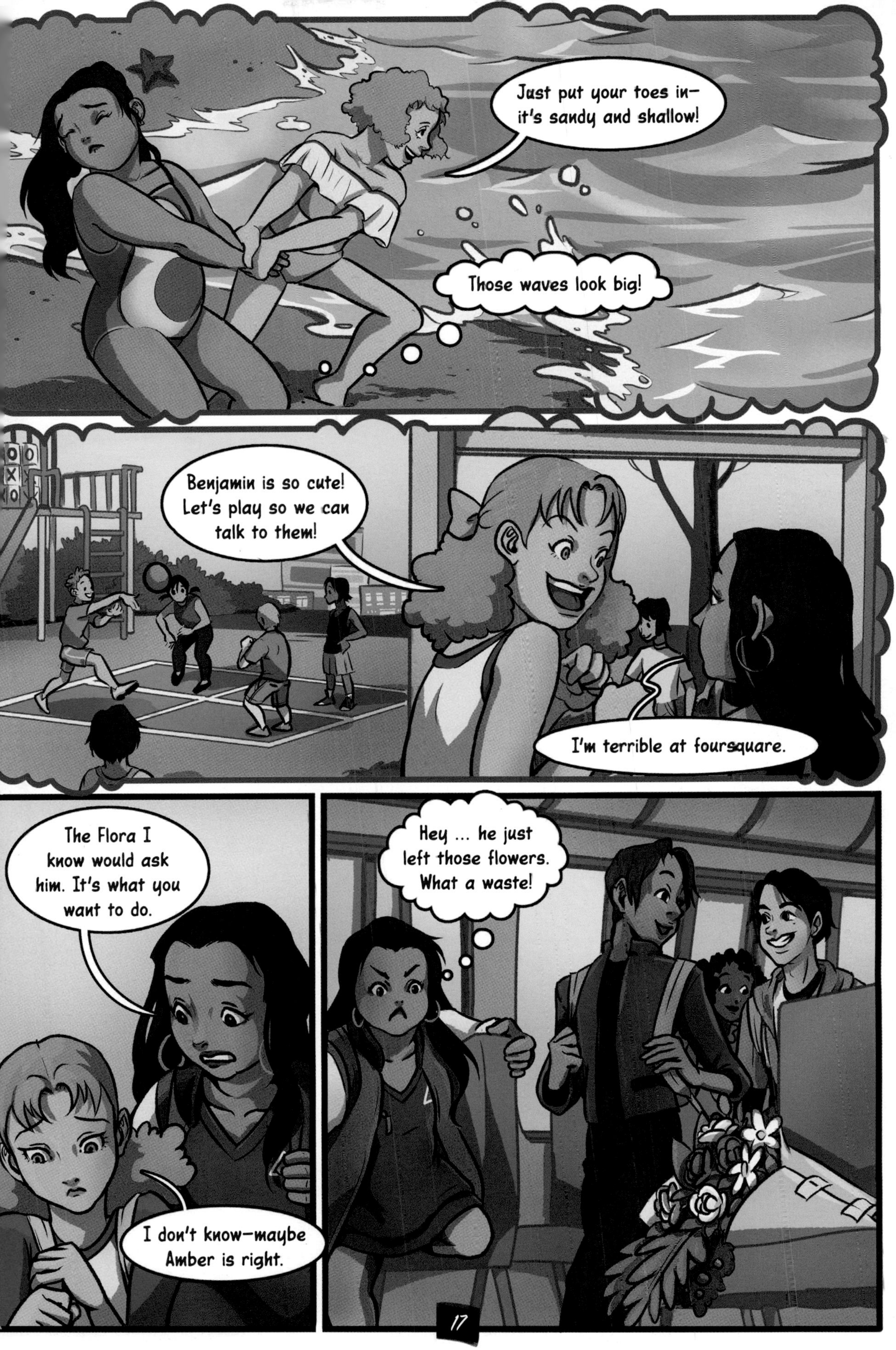
Just put your toes in—it's sandy and shallow!
Those waves look big!
Benjamin is so cute! Let's play so we can talk to them!
I'm terrible at foursquare.
The Flora I know would ask him. It's what you want to do.
I don't know—maybe Amber is right.
Hey ... he just left those flowers. What a waste!

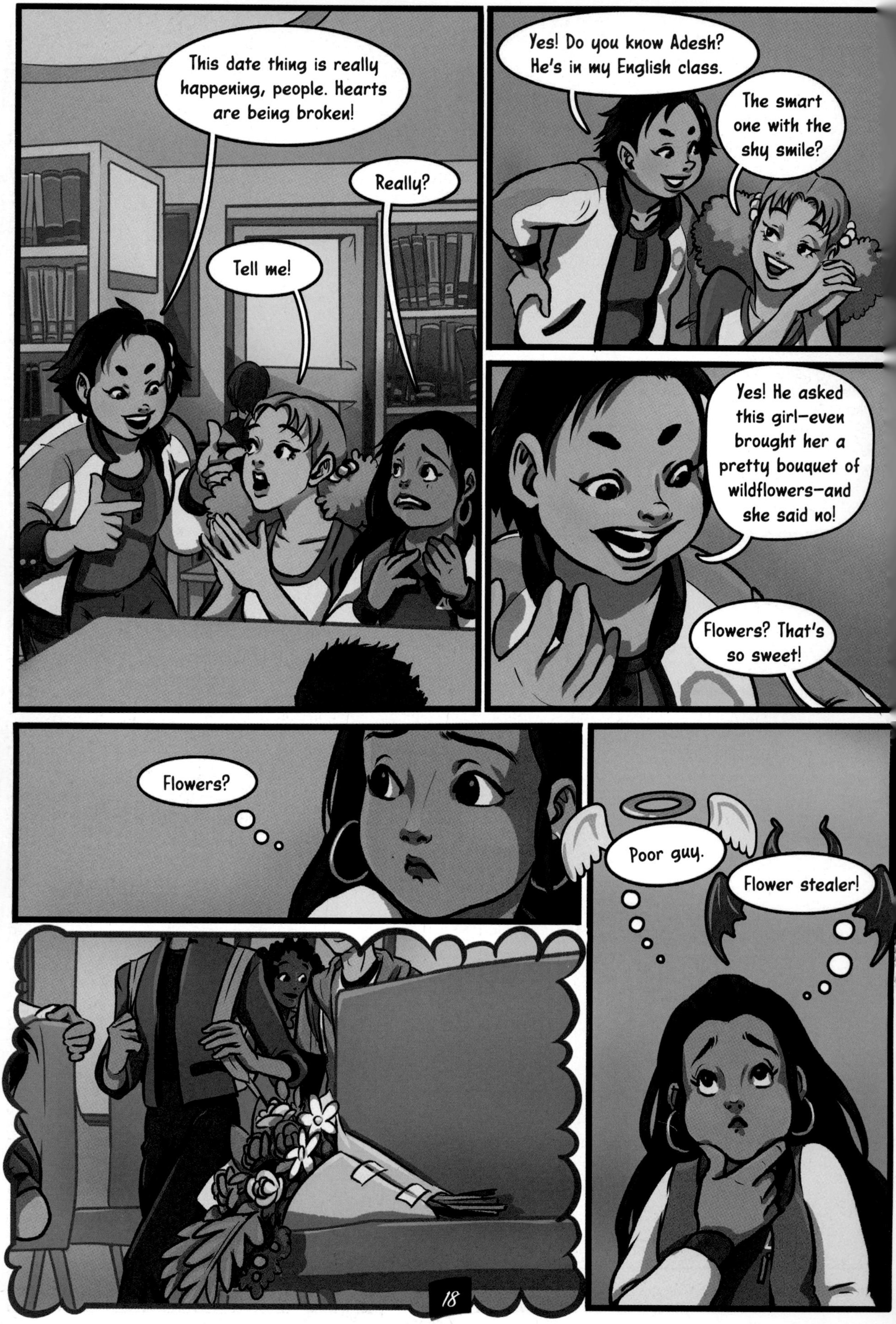

This date thing is really happening, people. Hearts are being broken!
Tell me!
Really?
Yes! Do you know Adesh? He's in my English class.
The smart one with the shy smile?
Yes! He asked this girl—even brought her a pretty bouquet of wildflowers—and she said no!
Flowers? That's so sweet!
Flowers?
Poor guy.
Flower stealer!

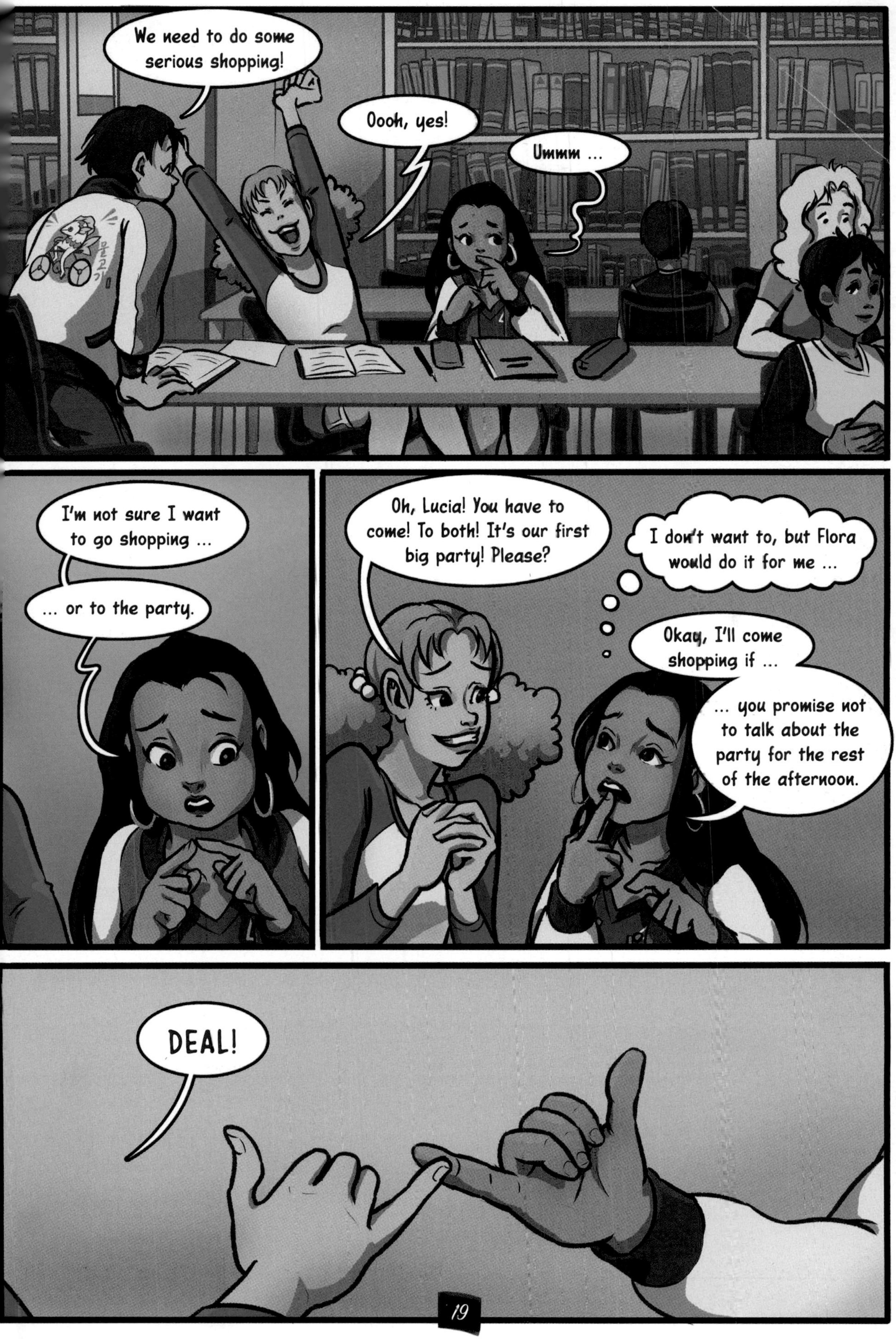
We need to do some serious shopping!
Oooh, yes!
Ummm ...
I'm not sure I want to go shopping ...
... or to the party.
Oh, Lucia! You have to come! To both! It's our first big party! Please?
I don't want to, but Flora would do it for me ...
Okay, I'll come shopping if ...
... you promise not to talk about the party for the rest of the afternoon.
DEAL!

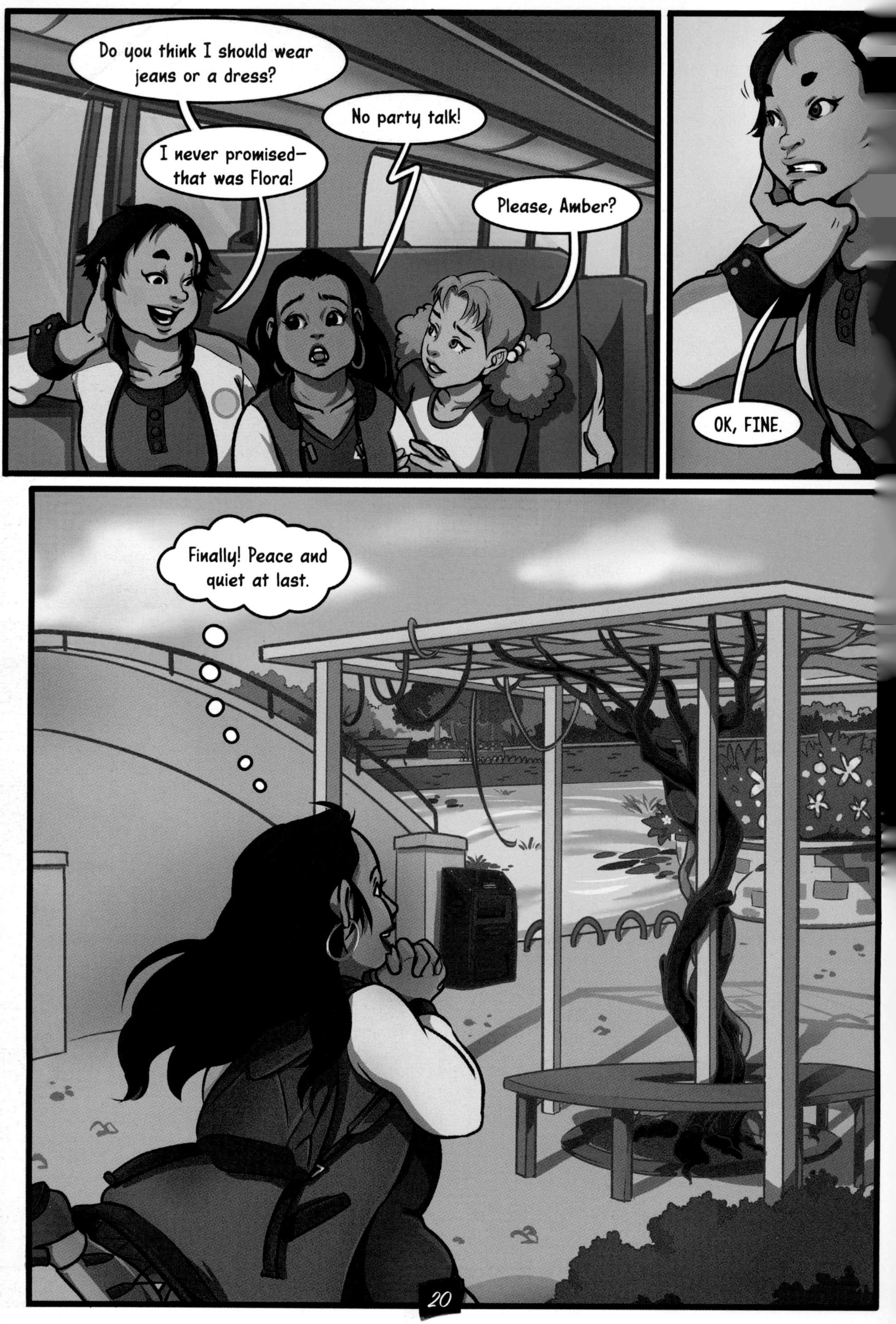

Do you think I should wear jeans or a dress?
I never promised— that was Flora!
No party talk!
Please, Amber?
OK, FINE.
Finally! Peace and quiet at last.

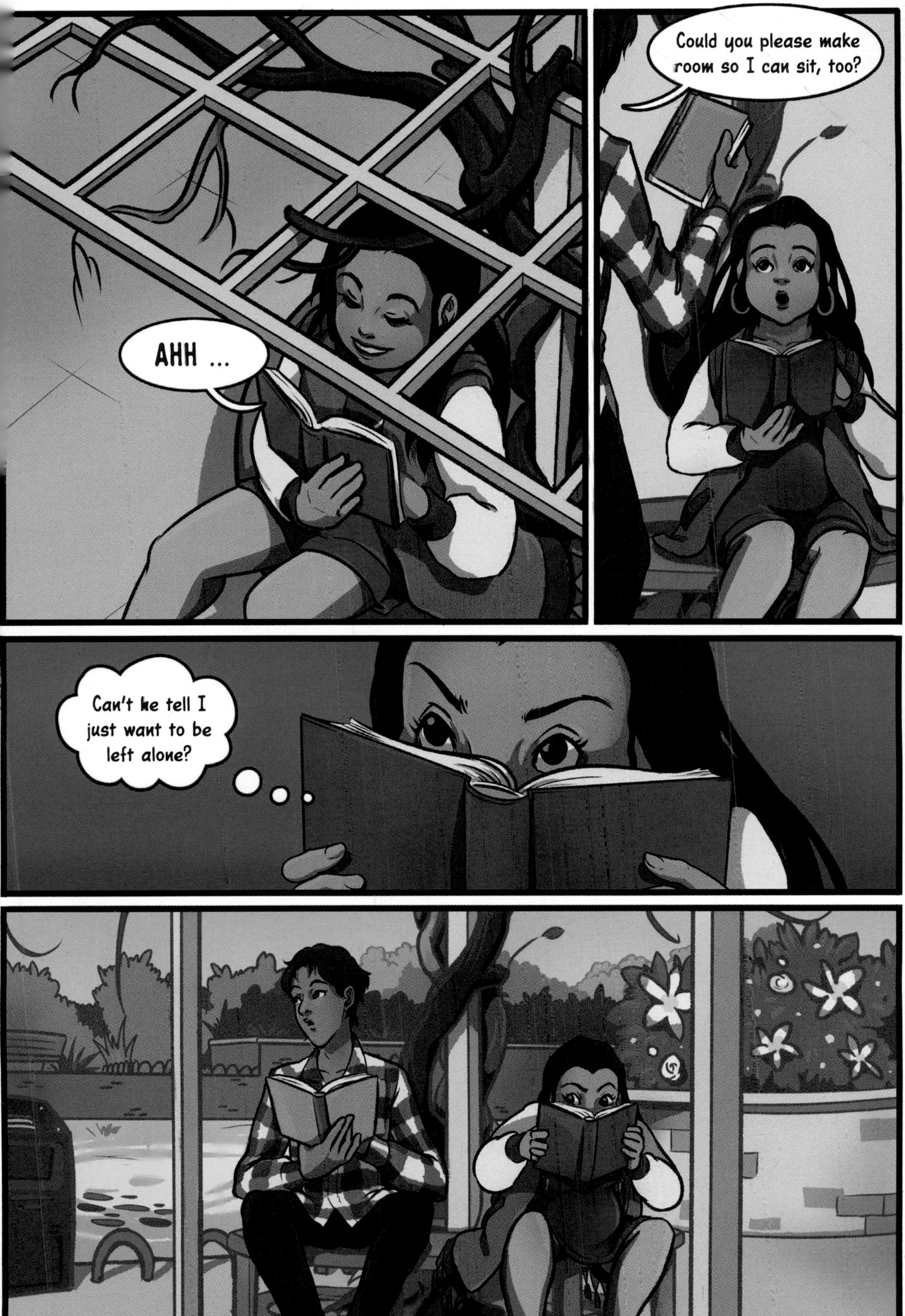
AHH ...
Could you please make room so I can sit, too?
Can't he tell I just want to be left alone?

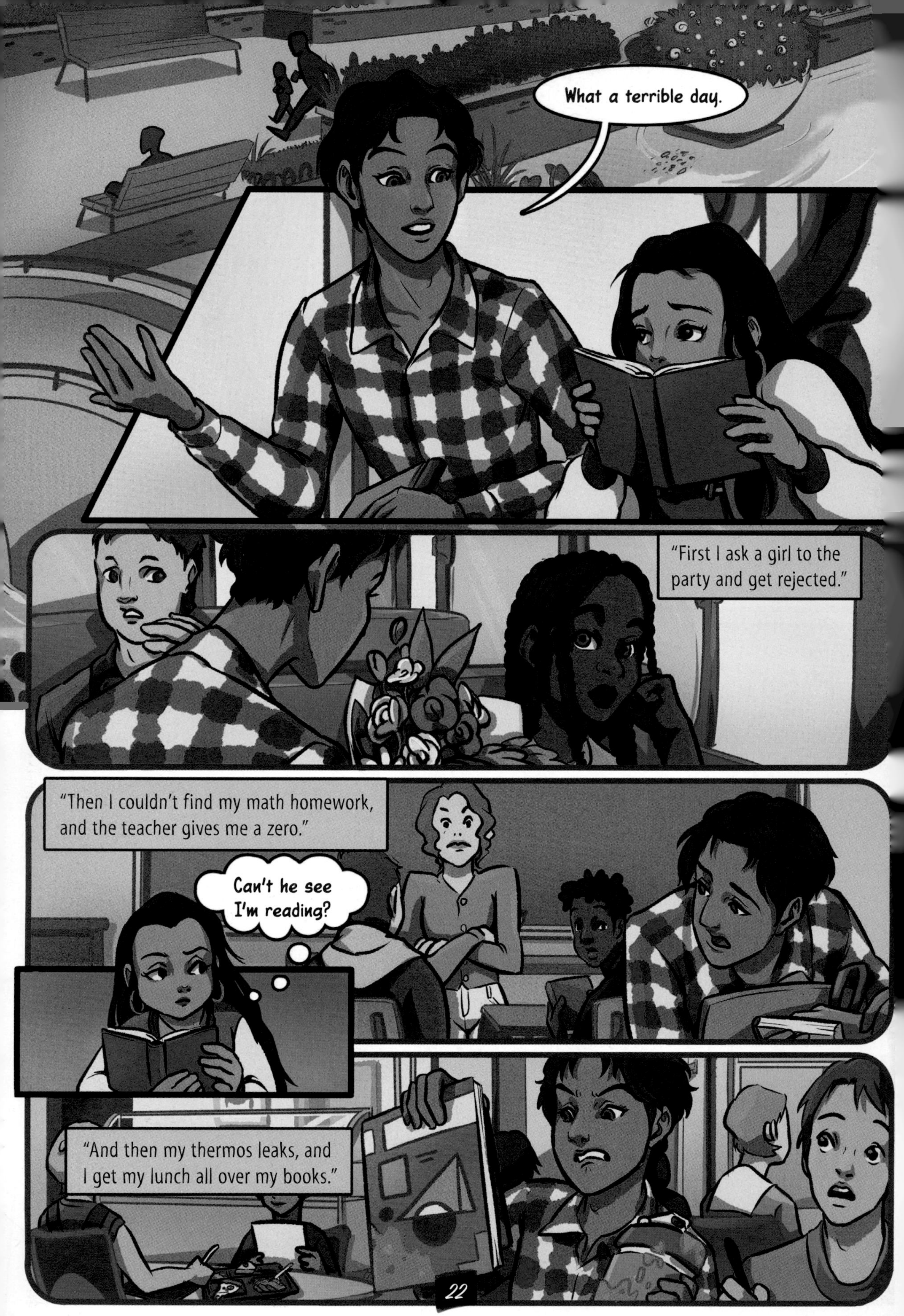
What a terrible day.
"First I ask a girl to the party and get rejected."
"Then I couldn't find my math homework, and the teacher gives me a zero."
Can't he see I'm reading?
"And then my thermos leaks, and I get my lunch all over my books."

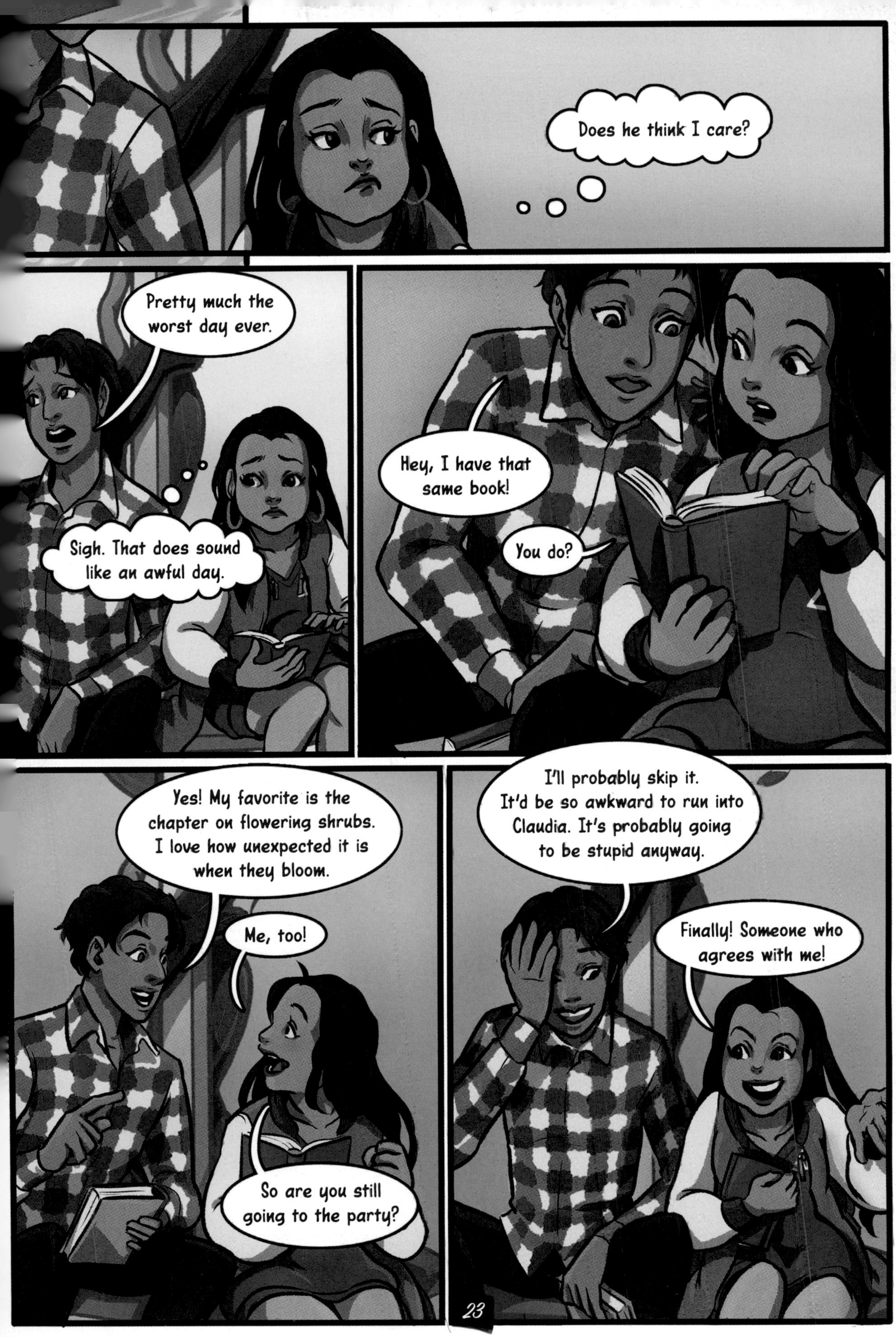

Does he think I care?
Pretty much the worst day ever.
Sigh. That does sound like an awful day.
Hey, I have that same book!
You do?
Yes! My favorite is the chapter on flowering shrubs. I love how unexpected it is when they bloom.
Me, too!
So are you still going to the party?
I'll probably skip it. It'd be so awkward to run into Claudia. It's probably going to be stupid anyway.
Finally! Someone who agrees with me!

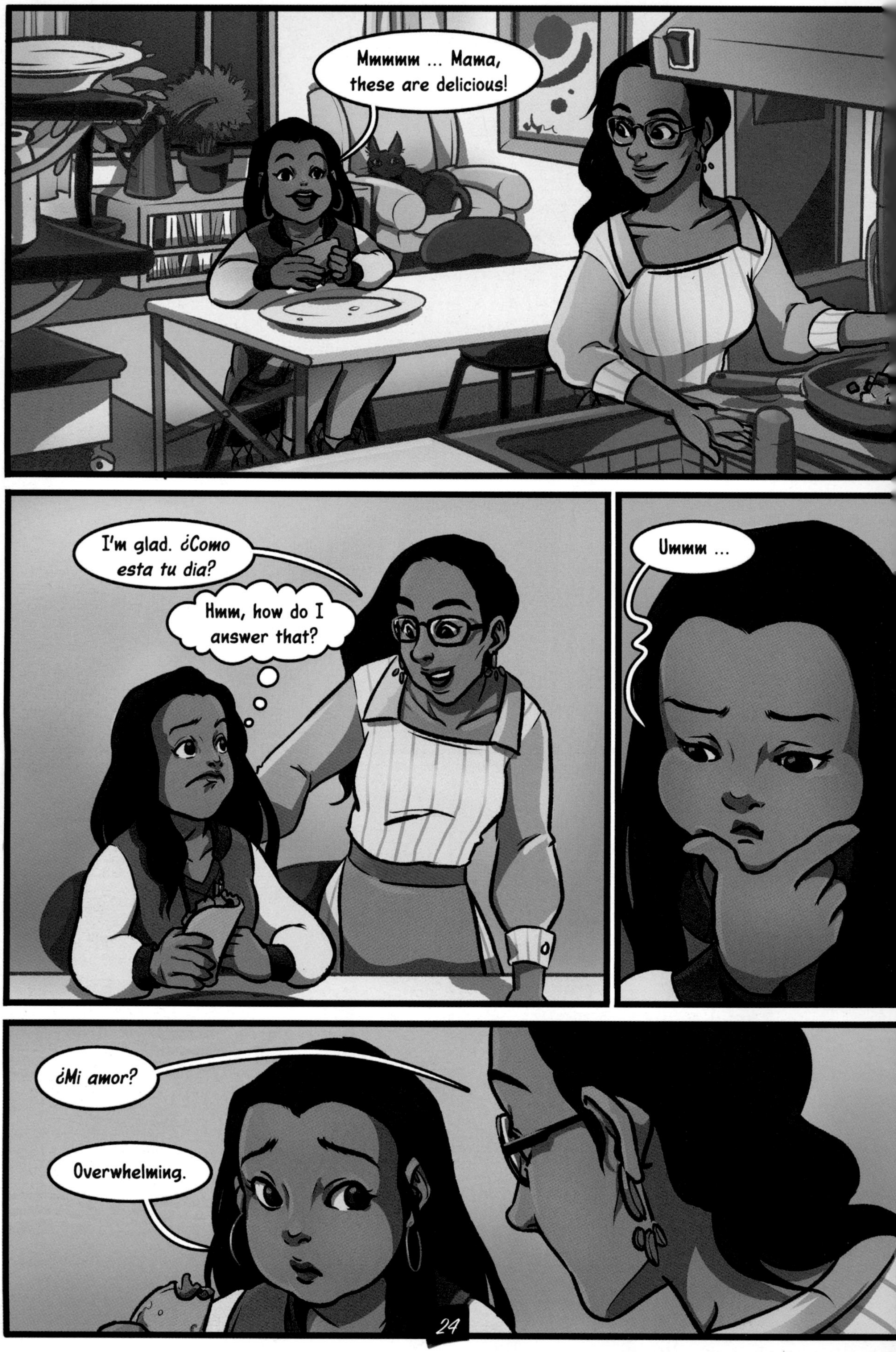

Mmmmm ... Mama, these are delicious!
I'm glad. ¿Como esta tu dia?
Hmm, how do I answer that?
Ummm ...
¿Mi amor?
Overwhelming.

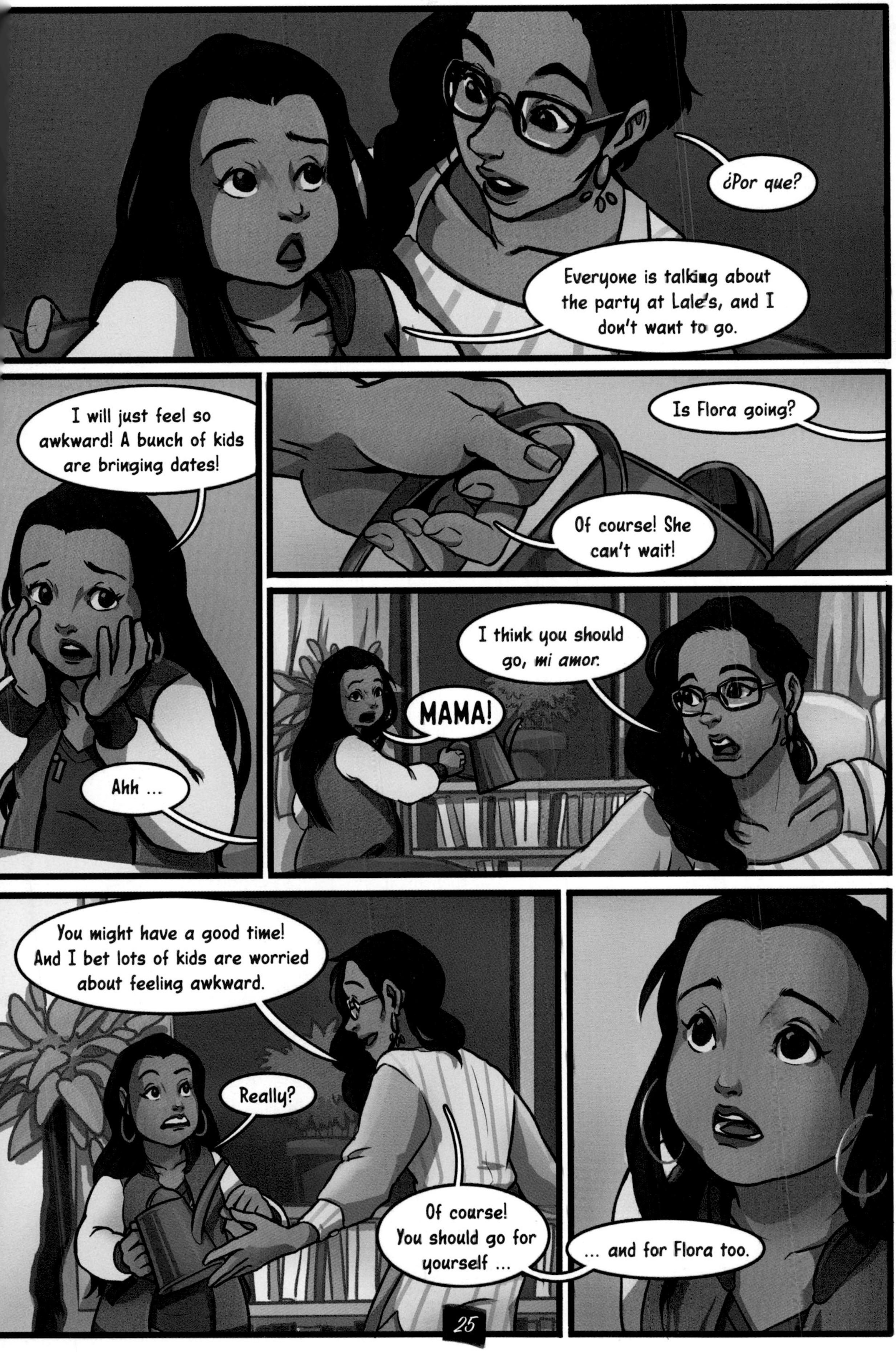

¿Por que?
Everyone is talking about the party at Lale's, and I don't want to go.
I will just feel so awkward! A bunch of kids are bringing dates!
Ahh ...
Is Flora going?
Of course! She can't wait!
I think you should go, *mi amor*.
MAMA!
You might have a good time! And I bet lots of kids are worried about feeling awkward.
Really?
Of course! You should go for yourself ...
... and for Flora too.

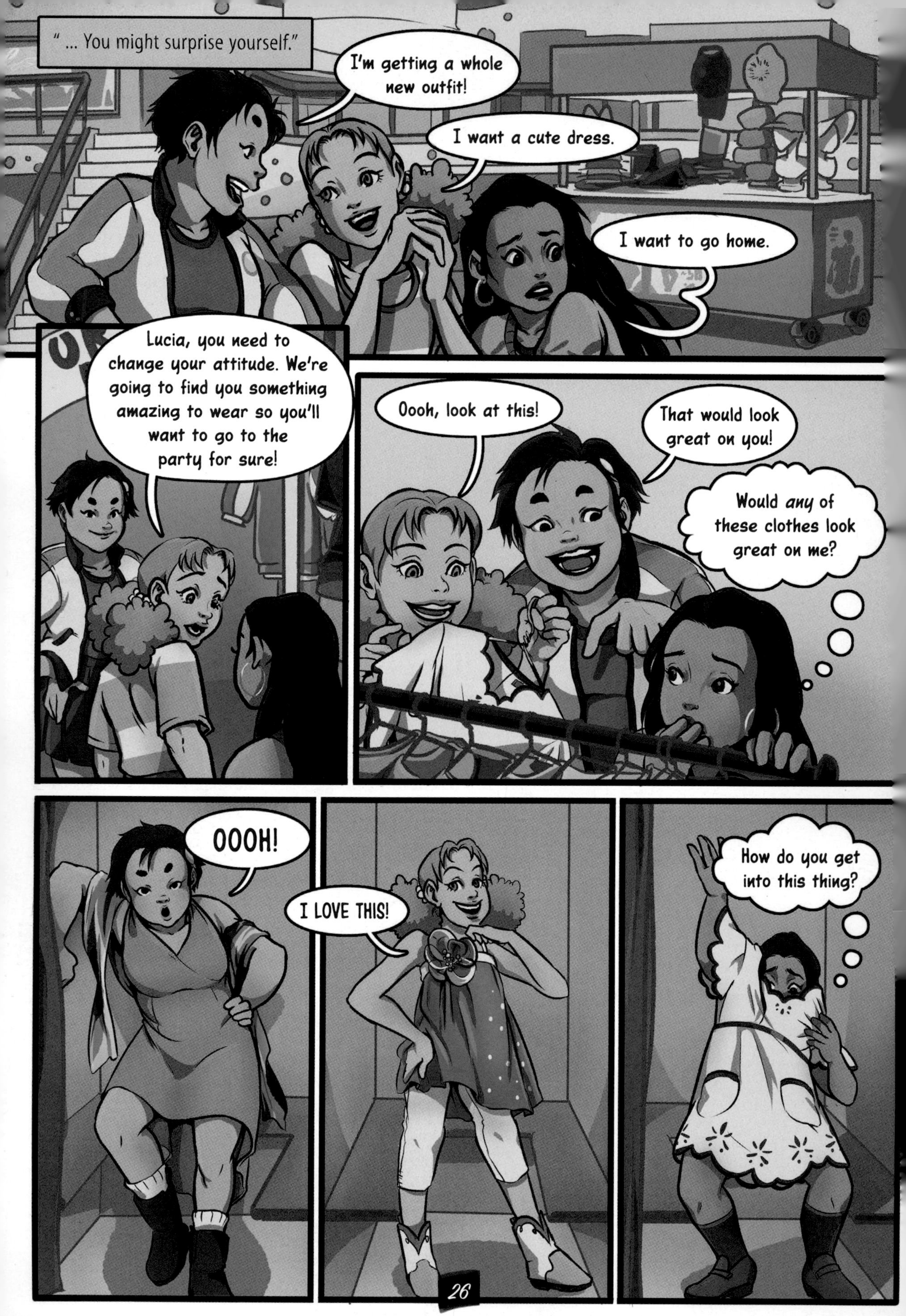
" ... You might surprise yourself."
I'm getting a whole new outfit!
I want a cute dress.
I want to go home.
Lucia, you need to change your attitude. We're going to find you something amazing to wear so you'll want to go to the party for sure!
Oooh, look at this!
That would look great on you!
Would *any* of these clothes look great on me?
OOOH!
I LOVE THIS!
How do you get into this thing?

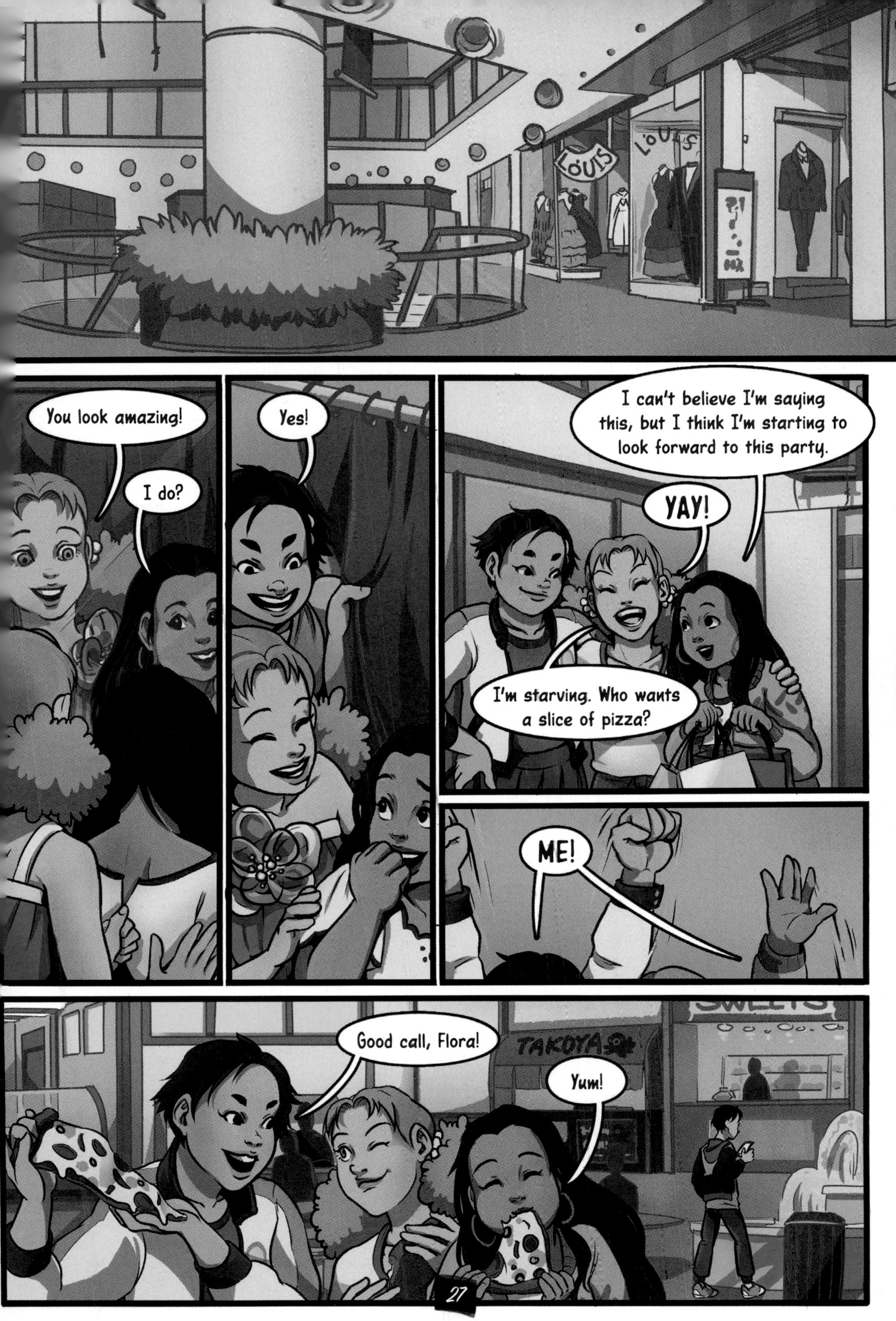
LOUIS
LOUIS
You look amazing!
I do?
Yes!
I can't believe I'm saying this, but I think I'm starting to look forward to this party.
YAY!
I'm starving. Who wants a slice of pizza?
ME!
SWEETS
TAKOYA
Good call, Flora!
Yum!

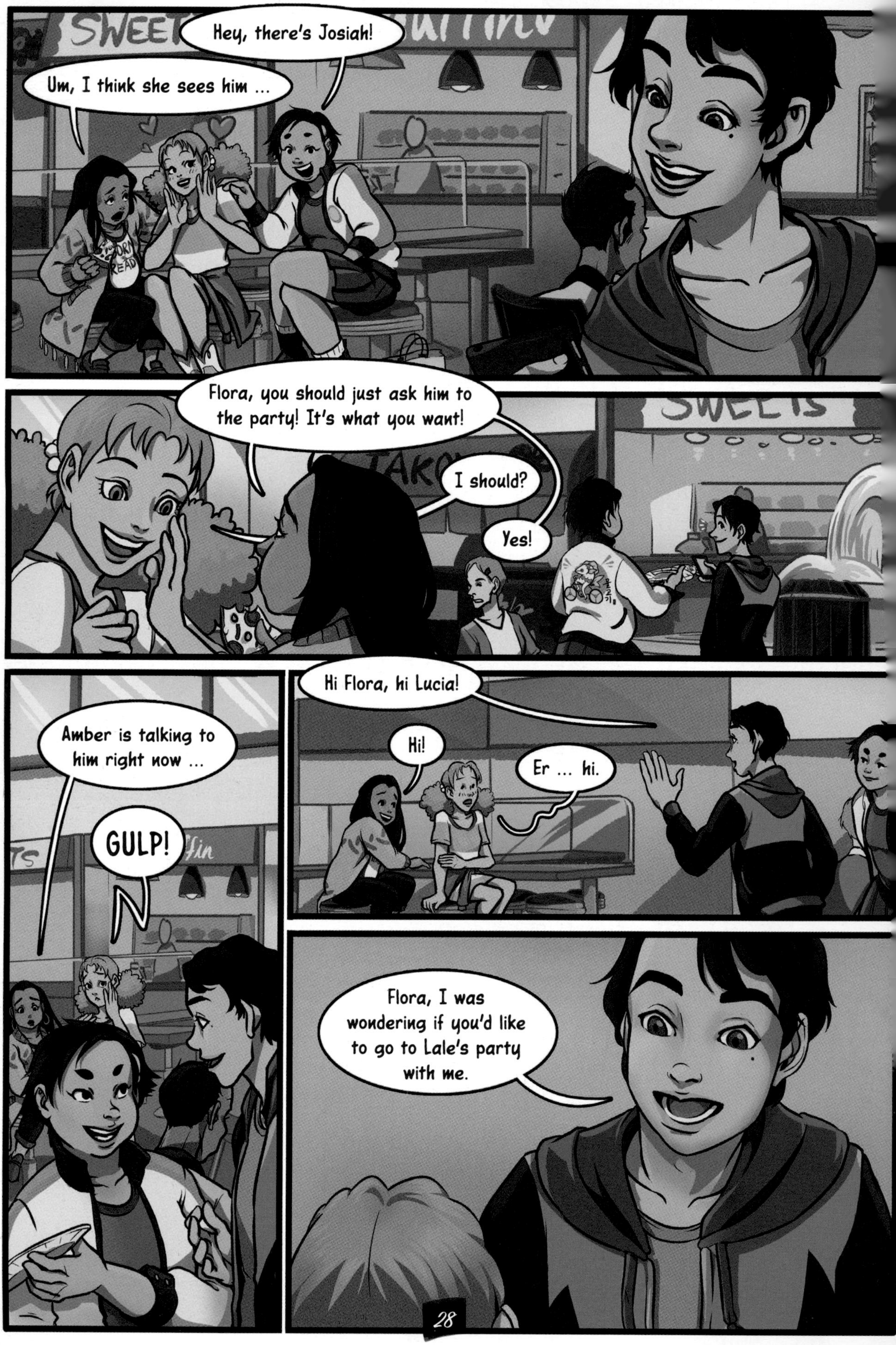
SWEET
Hey, there's Josiah!
Um, I think she sees him ...
BORN READ
Flora, you should just ask him to the party! It's what you want!
SWEETS
I should?
Yes!
Amber is talking to him right now ...
GULP!
Hi Flora, hi Lucia!
Hi!
Er ... hi.
Flora, I was wondering if you'd like to go to Lale's party with me.

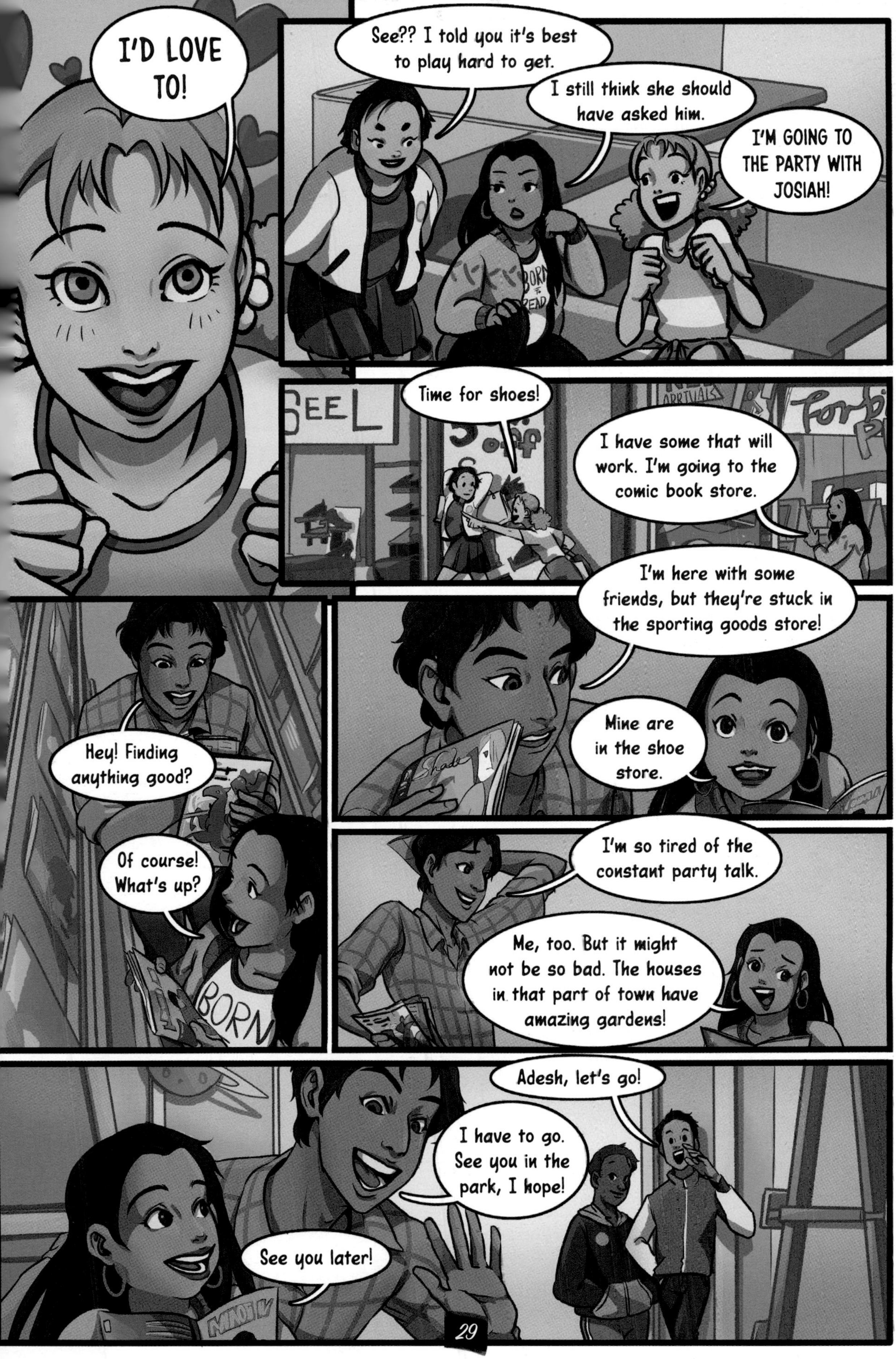
I'D LOVE TO!
See?? I told you it's best to play hard to get.
I still think she should have asked him.
I'M GOING TO THE PARTY WITH JOSIAH!
Time for shoes!
I have some that will work. I'm going to the comic book store.
Hey! Finding anything good?
Of course! What's up?
I'm here with some friends, but they're stuck in the sporting goods store!
Mine are in the shoe store.
I'm so tired of the constant party talk.
Me, too. But it might not be so bad. The houses in that part of town have amazing gardens!
Adesh, let's go!
I have to go. See you in the park, I hope!
See you later!

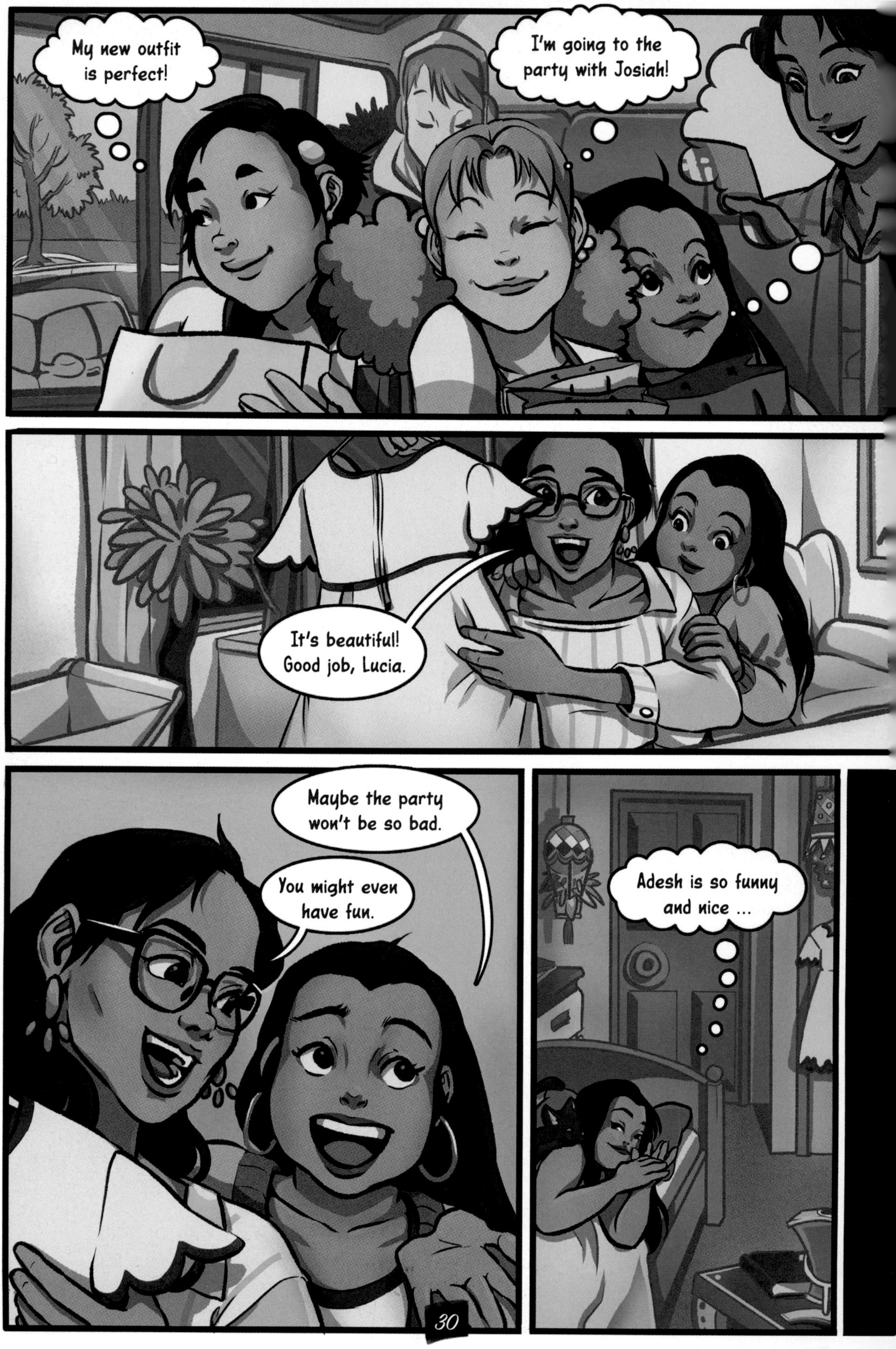

My new outfit is perfect!
I'm going to the party with Josiah!
It's beautiful! Good job, Lucia.
Maybe the party won't be so bad.
You might even have fun.
Adesh is so funny and nice ...

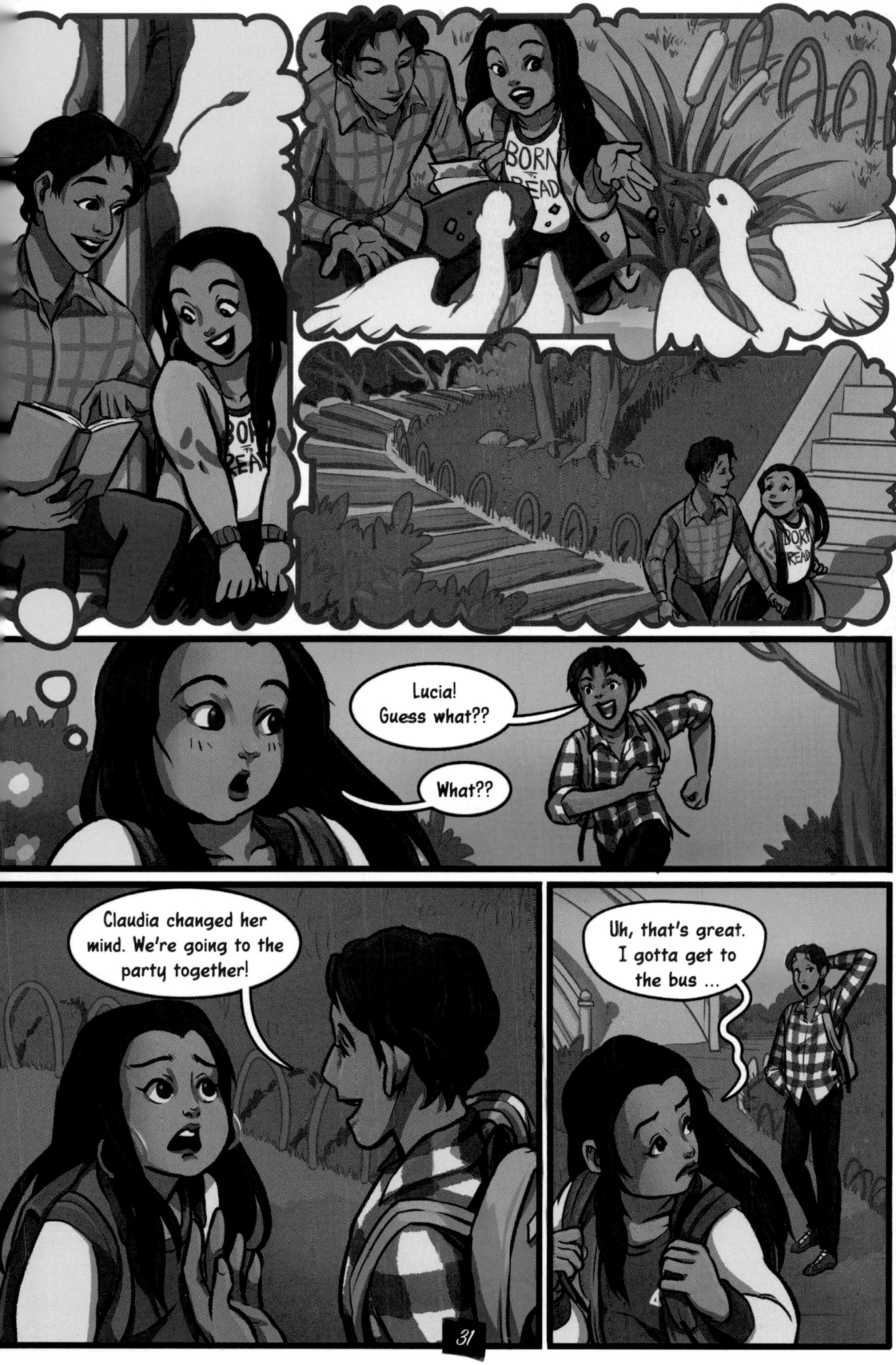
BORN TO READ
BORN TO READ
BORN TO READ
BORN TO READ
Lucia!
Guess what??
What??
Claudia changed her mind. We're going to the party together!
Uh, that's great. I gotta get to the bus ...

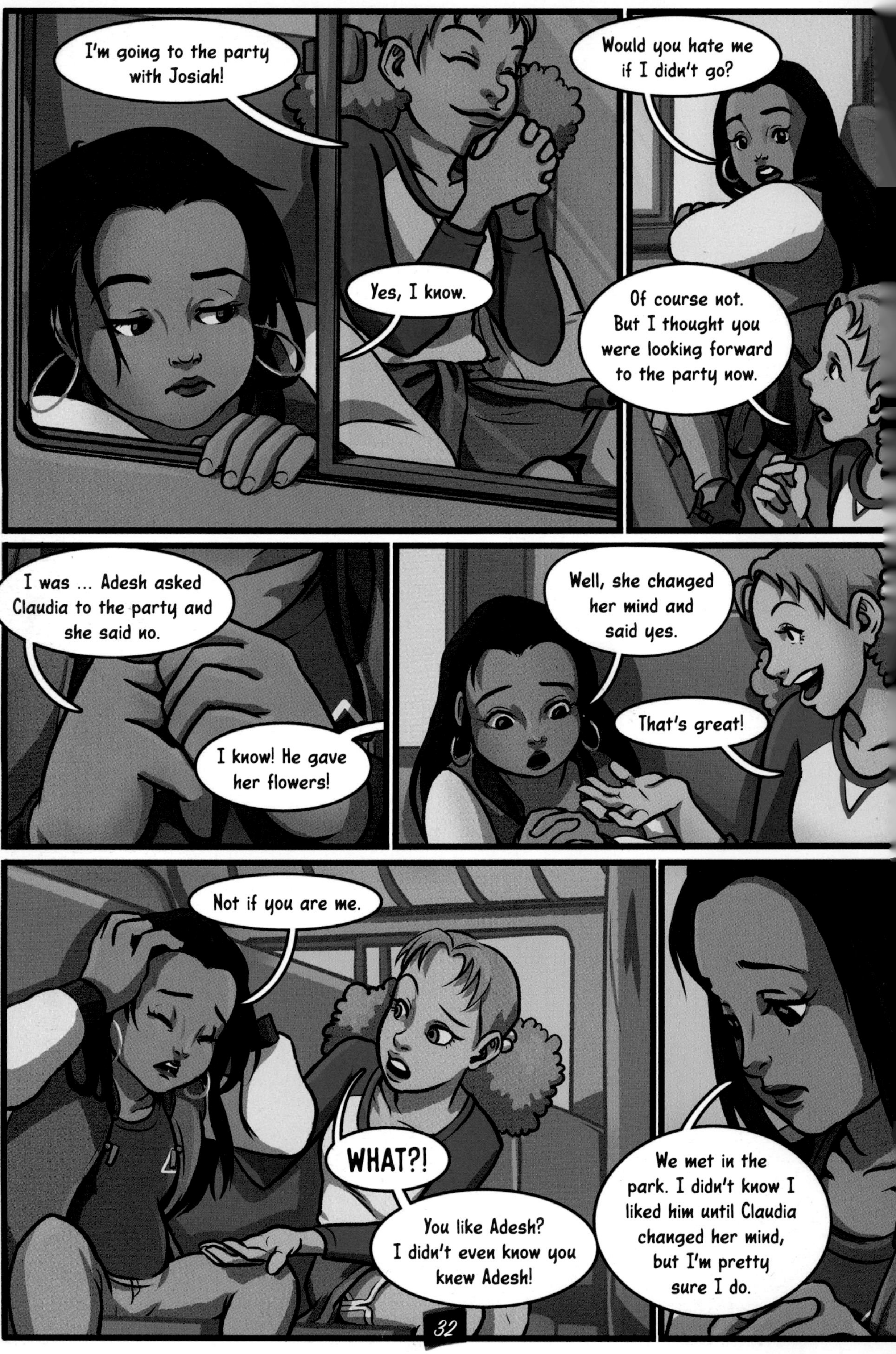

I'm going to the party with Josiah!
Yes, I know.
Would you hate me if I didn't go?
Of course not. But I thought you were looking forward to the party now.
I was ... Adesh asked Claudia to the party and she said no.
I know! He gave her flowers!
Well, she changed her mind and said yes.
That's great!
Not if you are me.
WHAT?!
You like Adesh? I didn't even know you knew Adesh!
We met in the park. I didn't know I liked him until Claudia changed her mind, but I'm pretty sure I do.

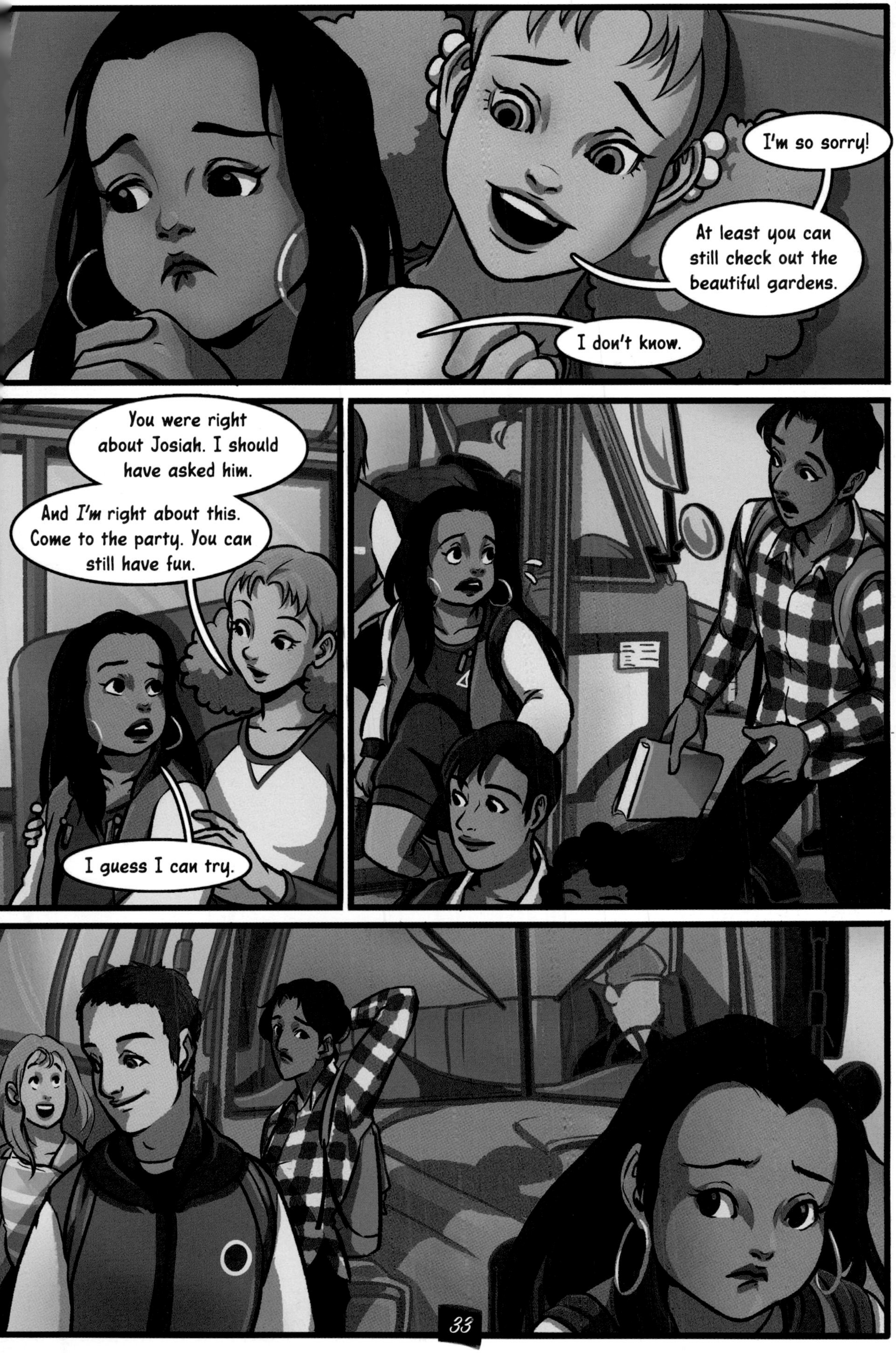
I'm so sorry!
At least you can still check out the beautiful gardens.
I don't know.
You were right about Josiah. I should have asked him.
And *I'm* right about this. Come to the party. You can still have fun.
I guess I can try.

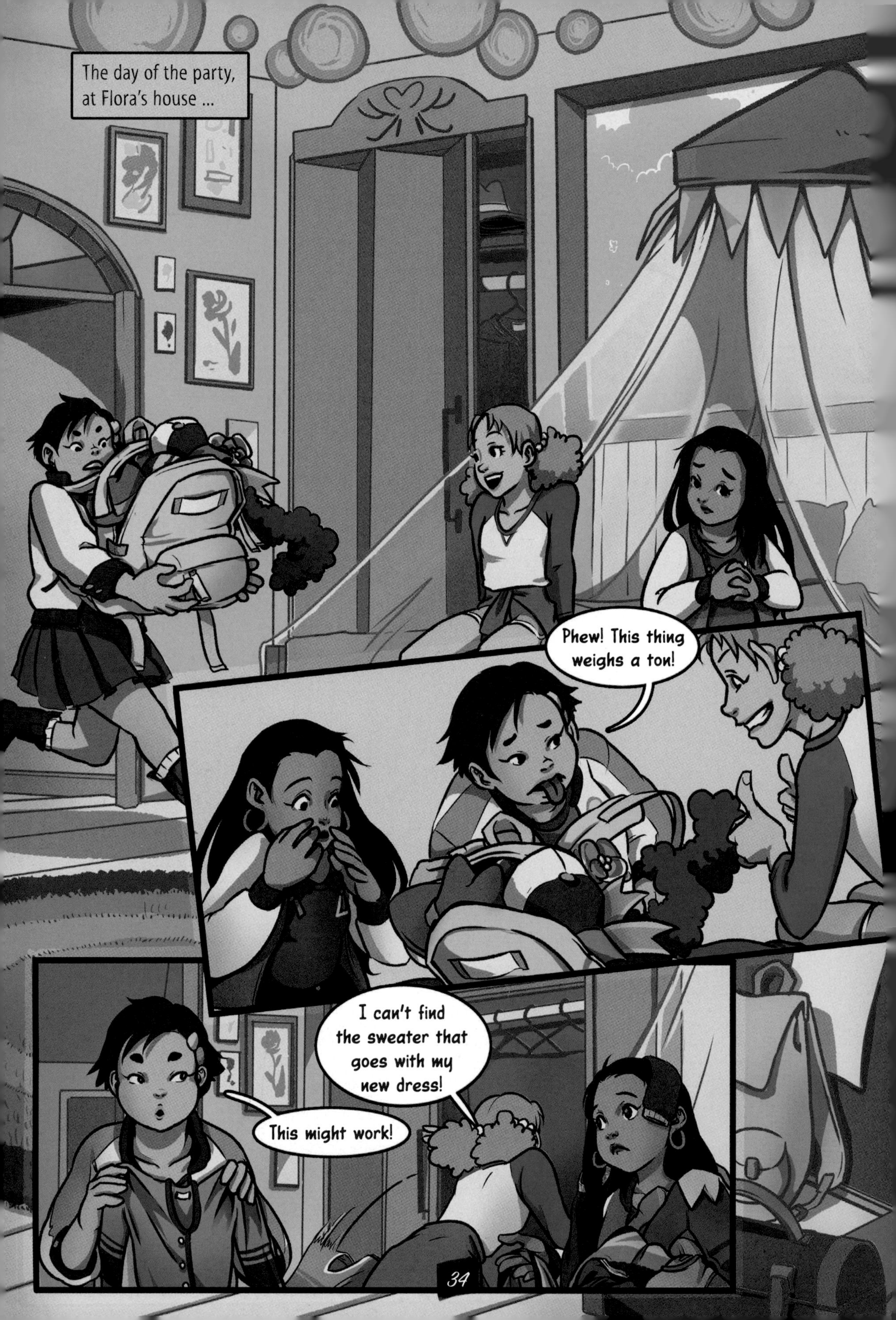
The day of the party, at Flora's house ...
Phew! This thing weighs a ton!
I can't find the sweater that goes with my new dress!
This might work!

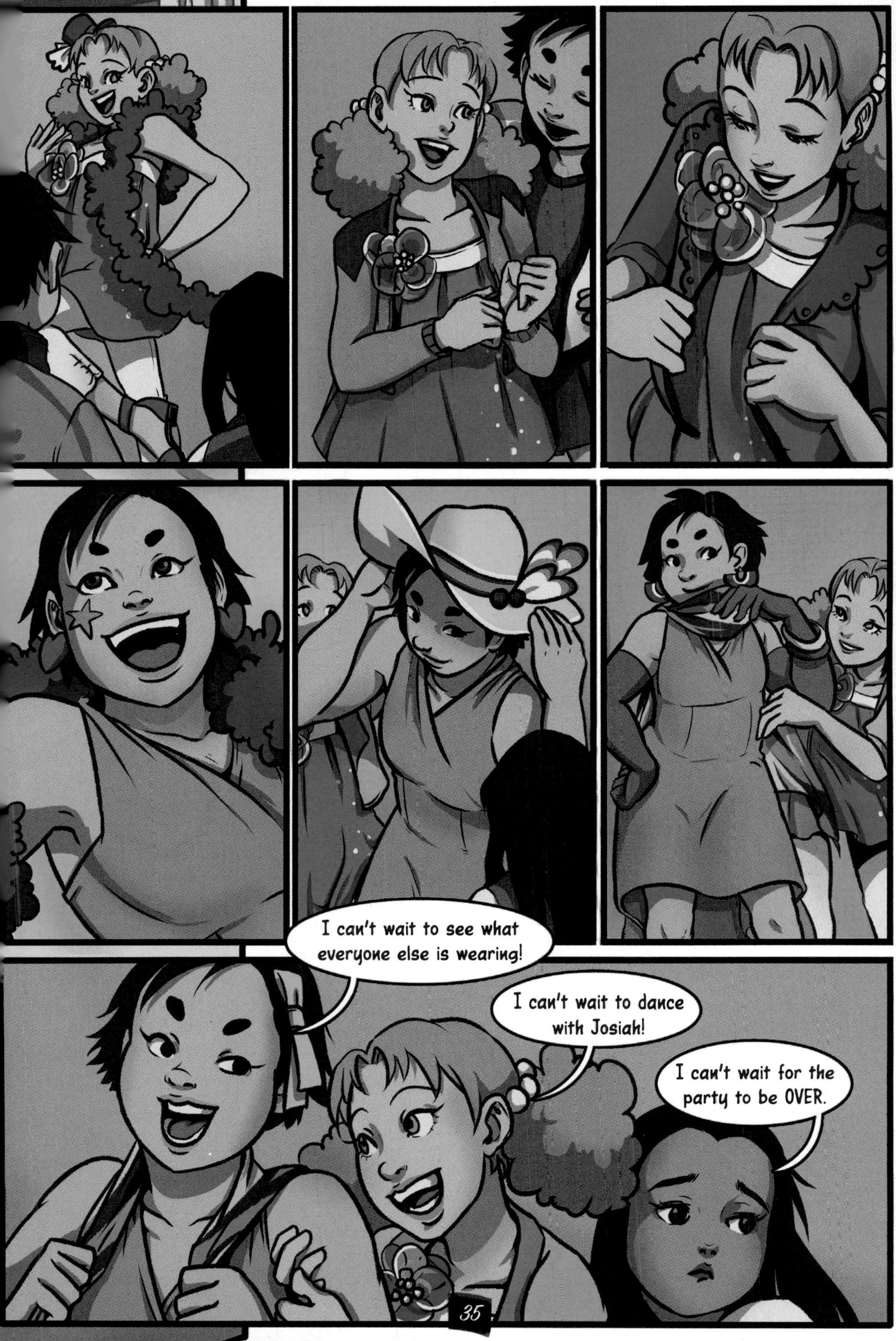
I can't wait to see what everyone else is wearing!
I can't wait to dance with Josiah!
I can't wait for the party to be OVER.

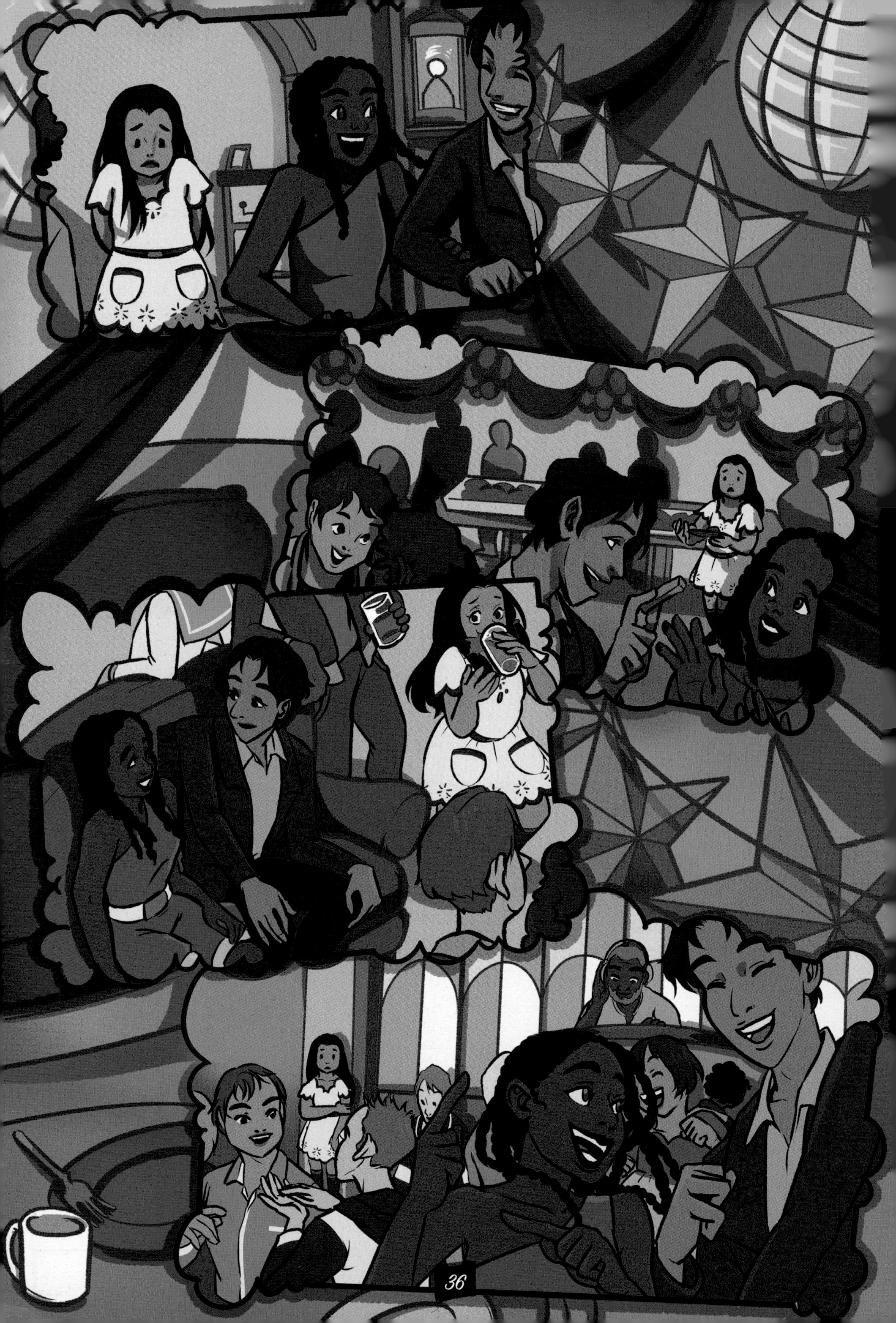

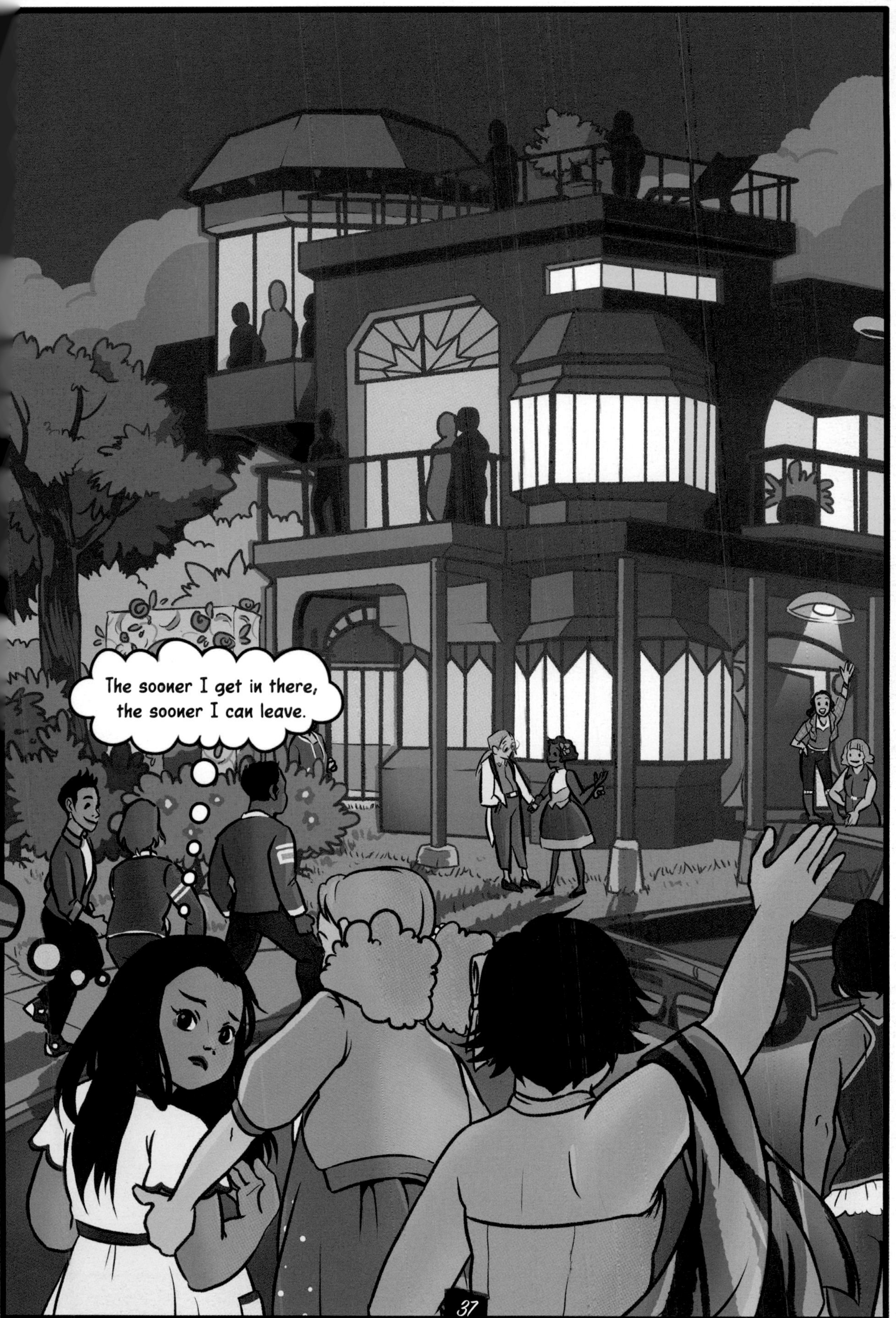
The sooner I get in there, the sooner I can leave.

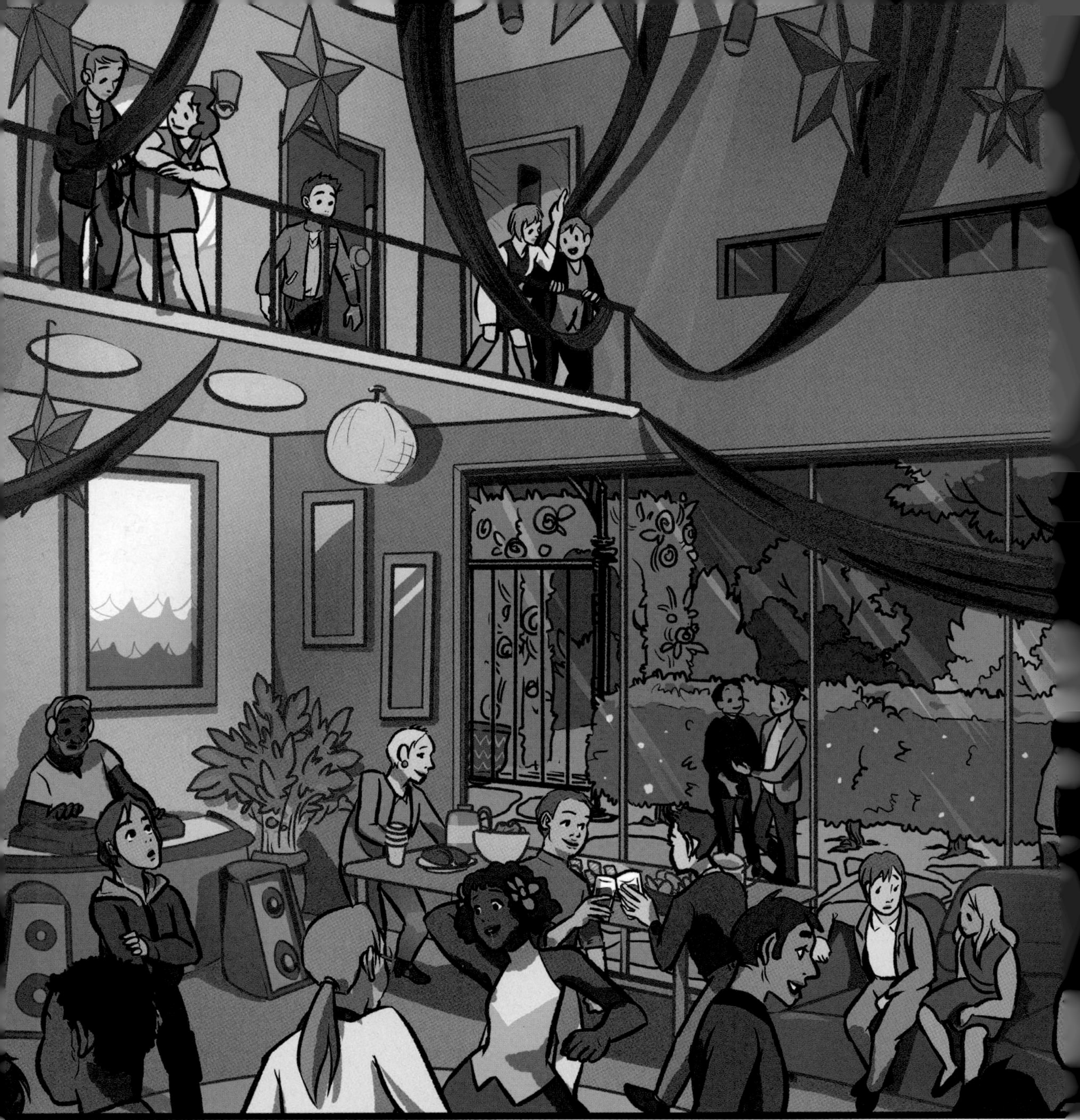

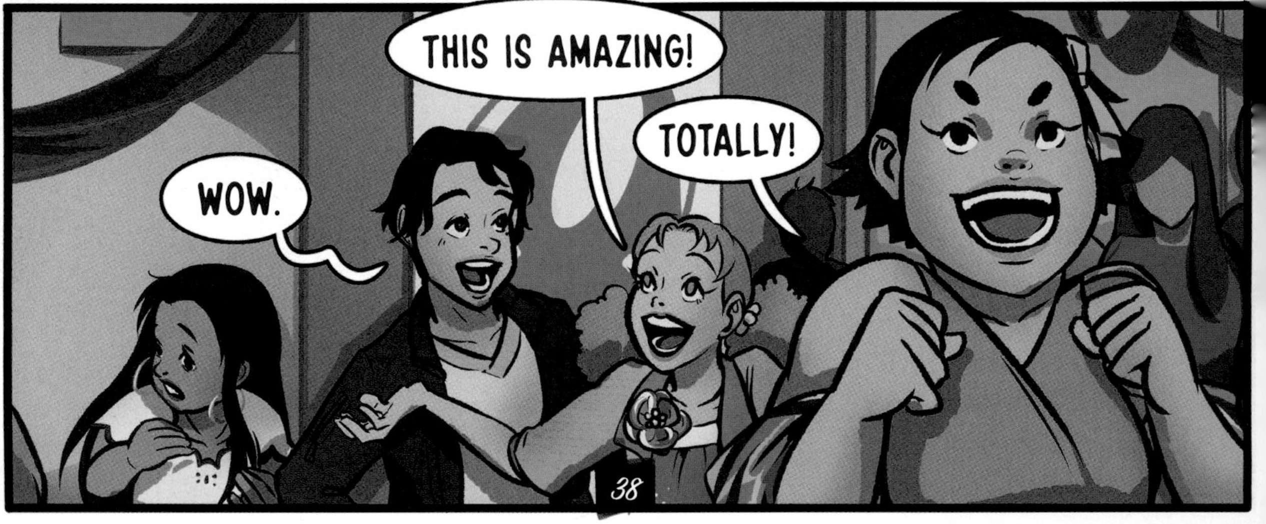
WOW.
THIS IS AMAZING!
TOTALLY!

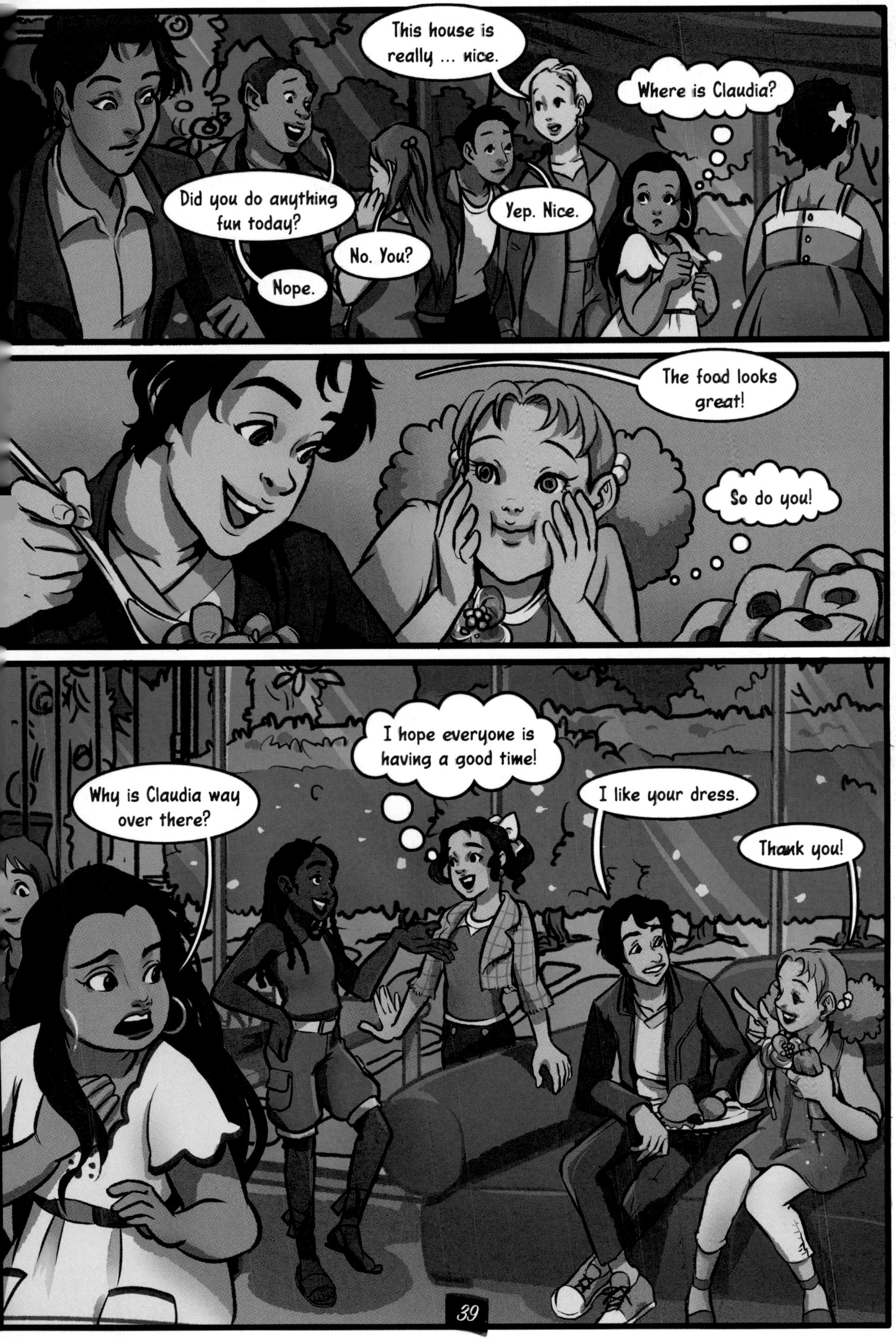
This house is really ... nice.
Where is Claudia?
Did you do anything fun today?
Yep. Nice.
No. You?
Nope.
The food looks great!
So do you!
I hope everyone is having a good time!
Why is Claudia way over there?
I like your dress.
Thank you!

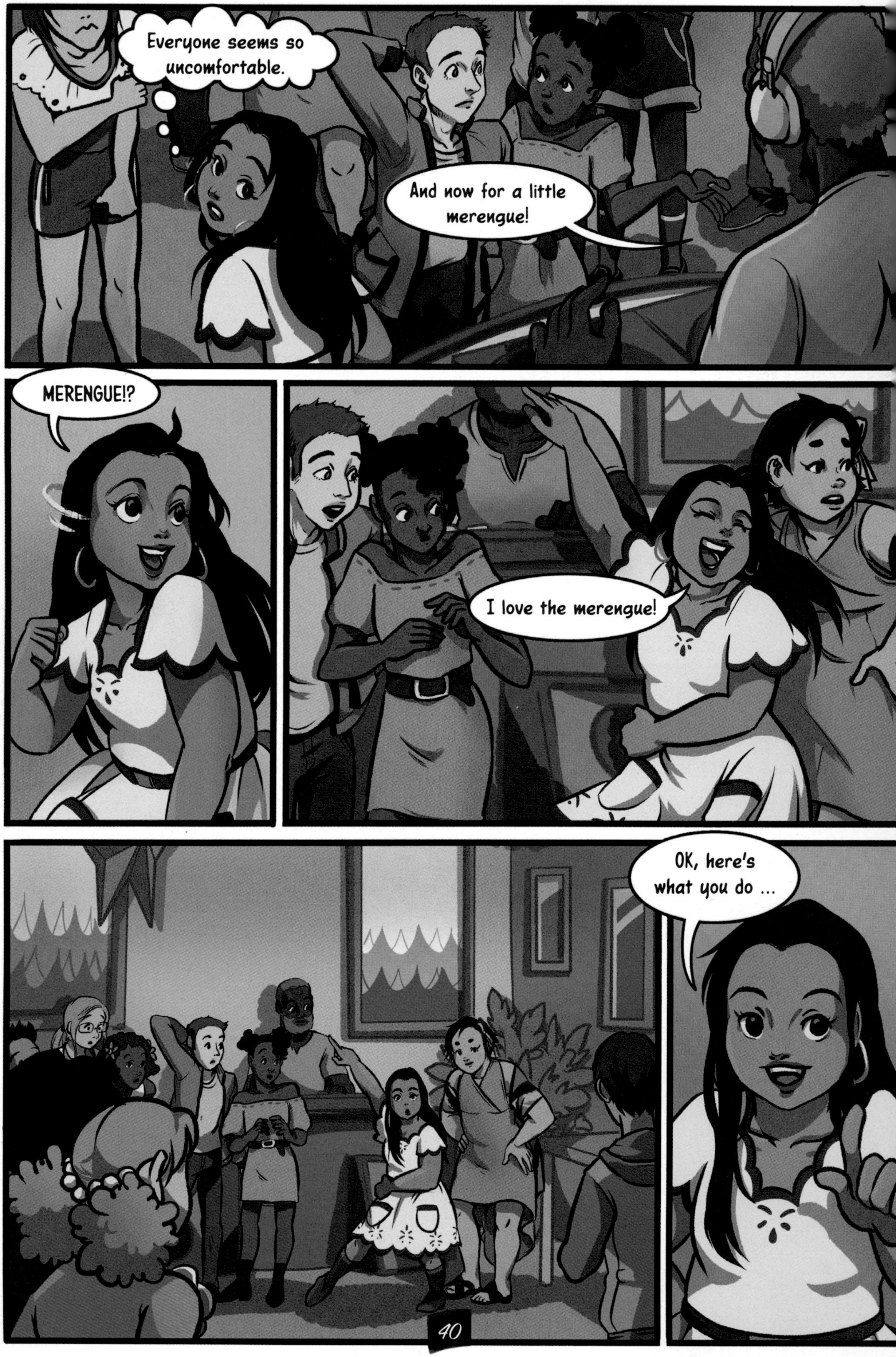
Everyone seems so uncomfortable.
And now for a little merengue!
MERENGUE!?
I love the merengue!
OK, here's what you do ...

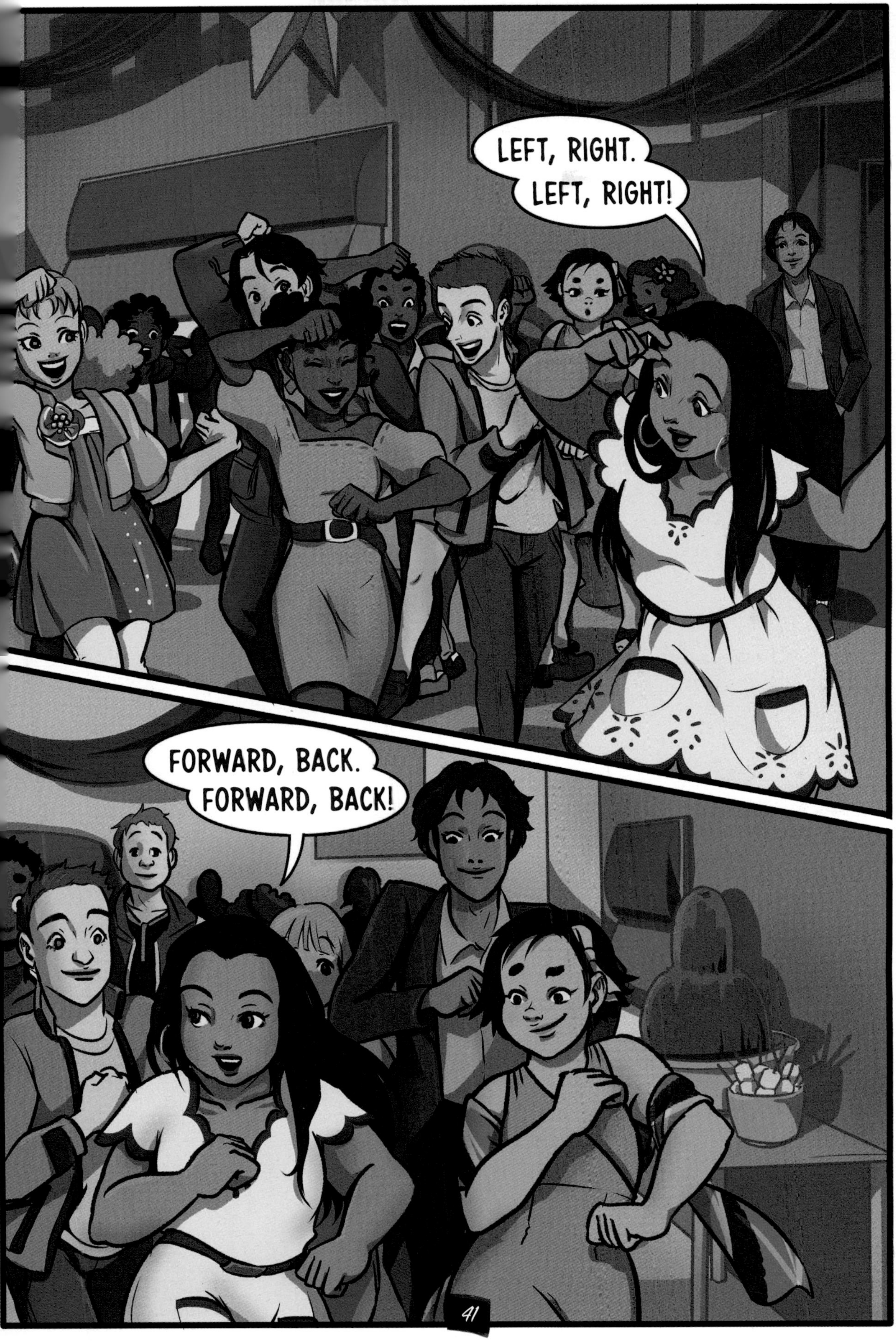
LEFT, RIGHT.
LEFT, RIGHT!
FORWARD, BACK.
FORWARD, BACK!

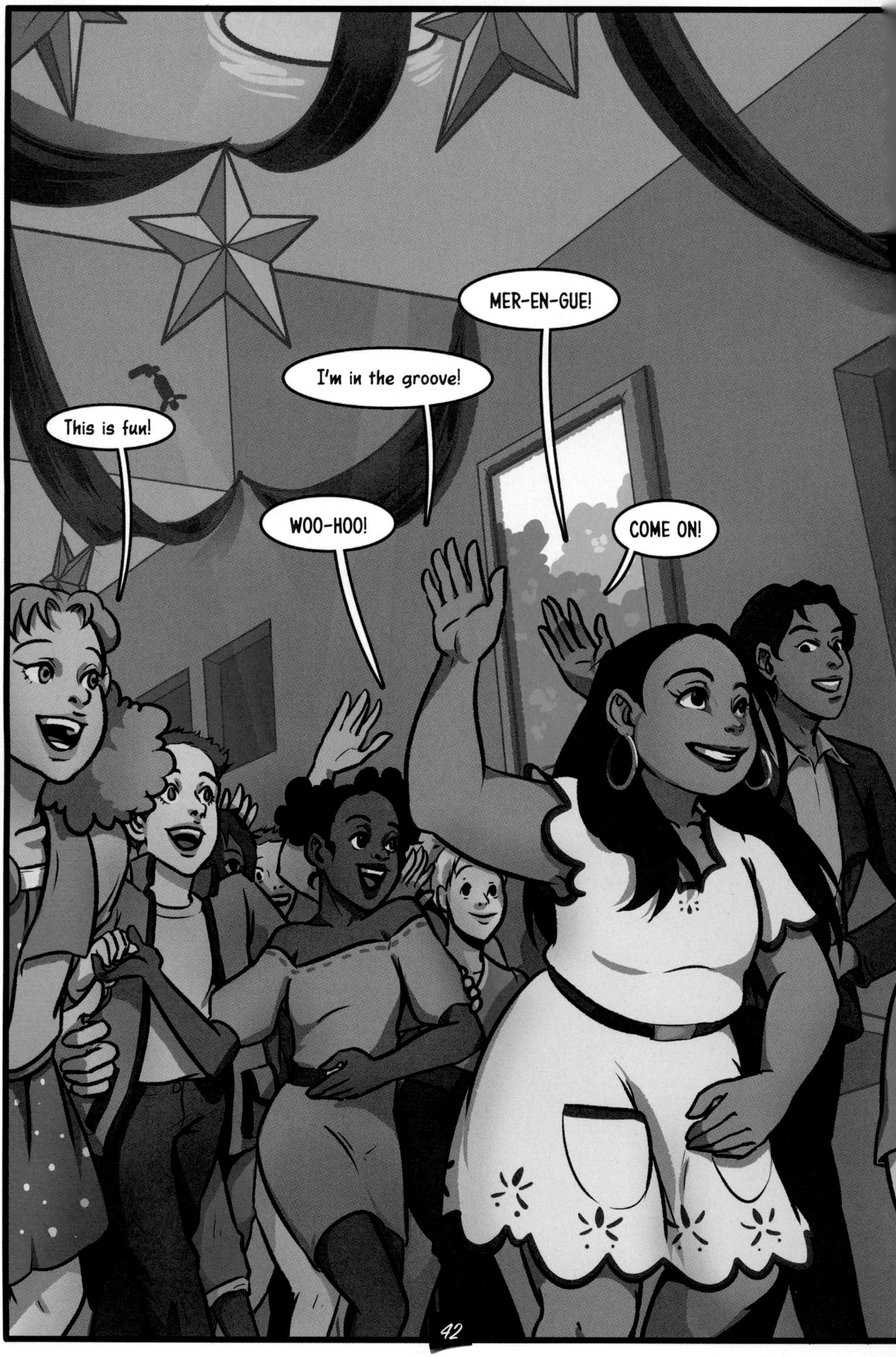

This is fun!
I'm in the groove!
MER-EN-GUE!
WOO-HOO!
COME ON!

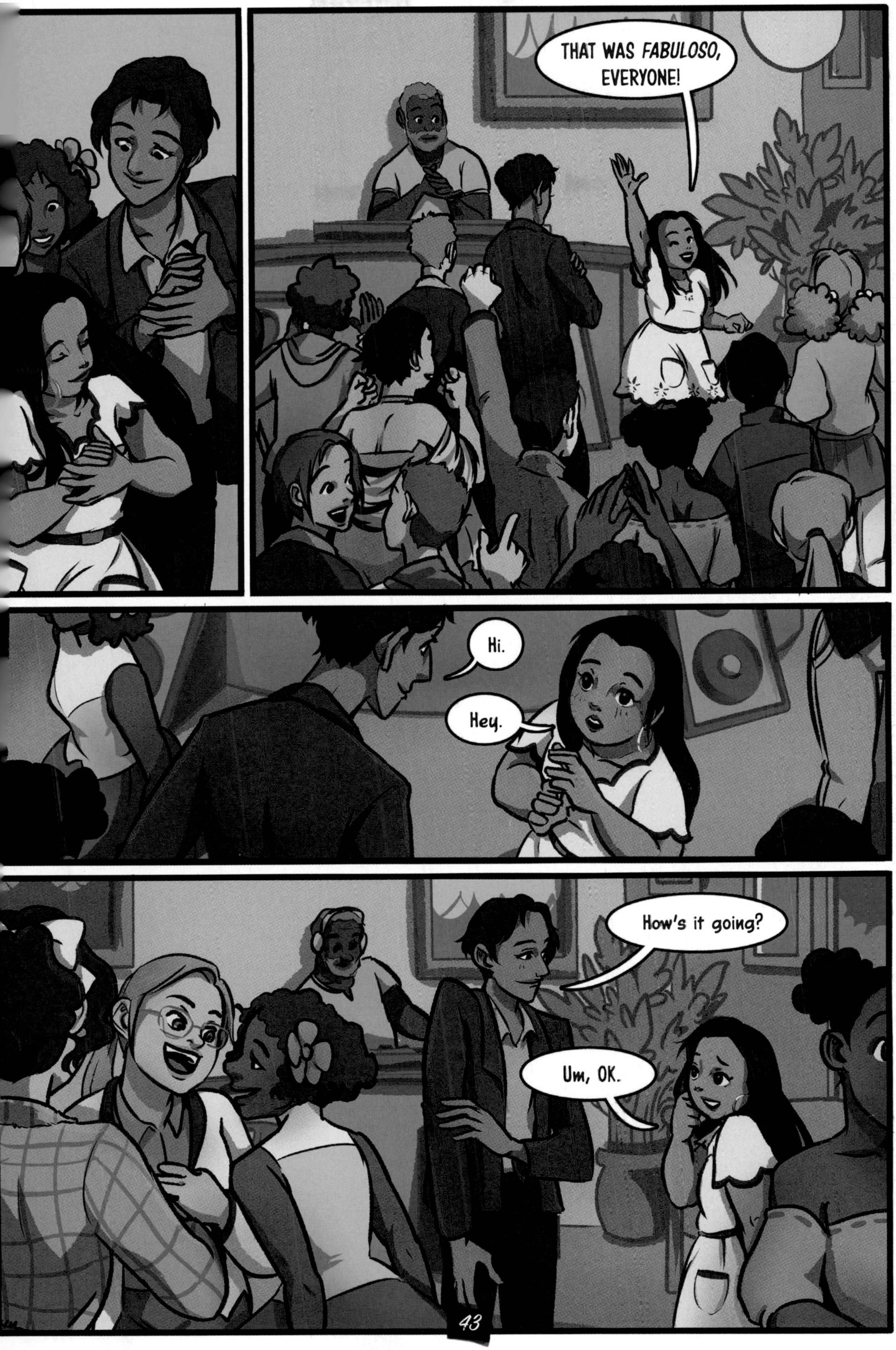
THAT WAS *FABULOSO*, EVERYONE!
Hi.
Hey.
How's it going?
Um, OK.

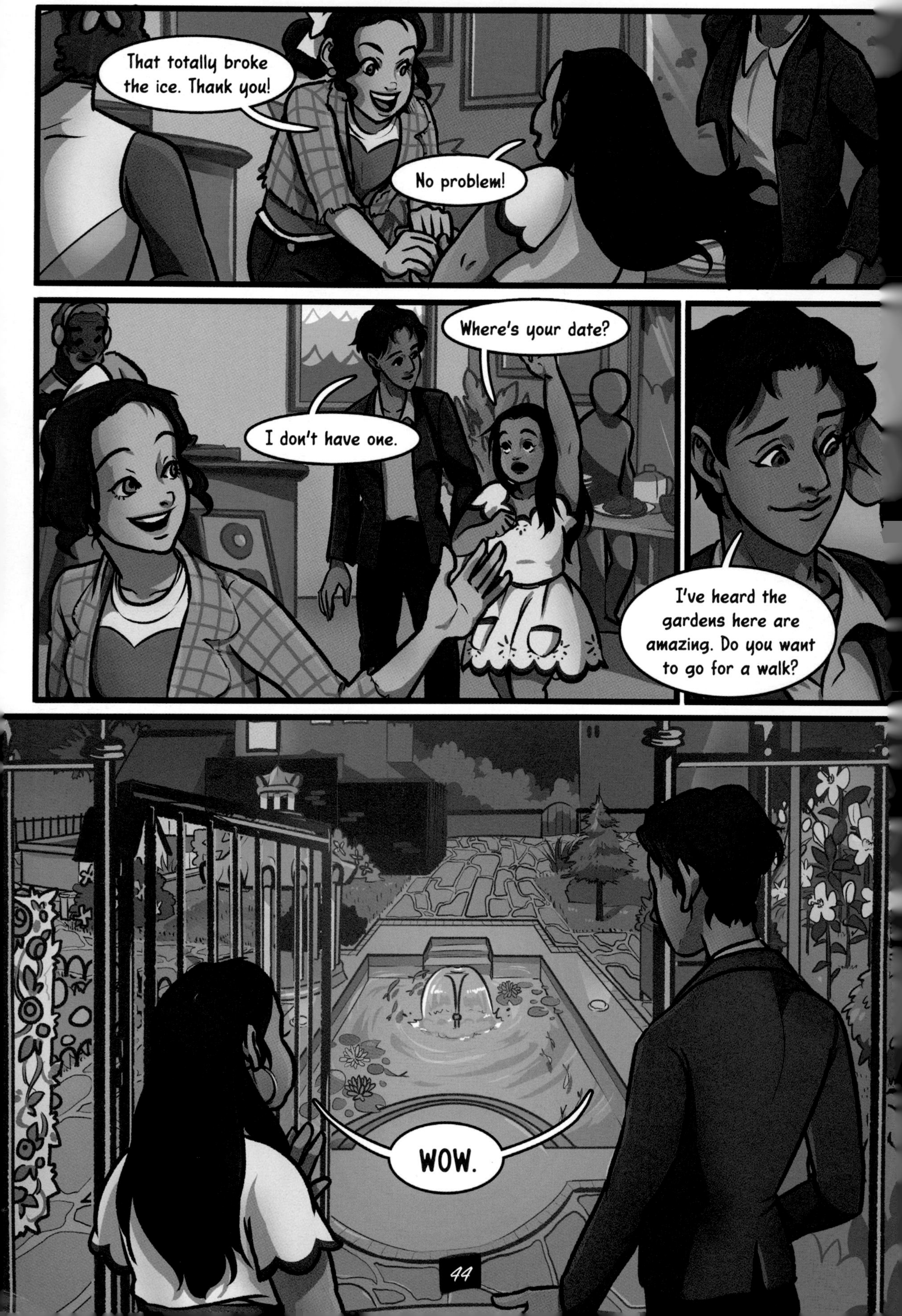
That totally broke the ice. Thank you!
No problem!
Where's your date?
I don't have one.
I've heard the gardens here are amazing. Do you want to go for a walk?
WOW.

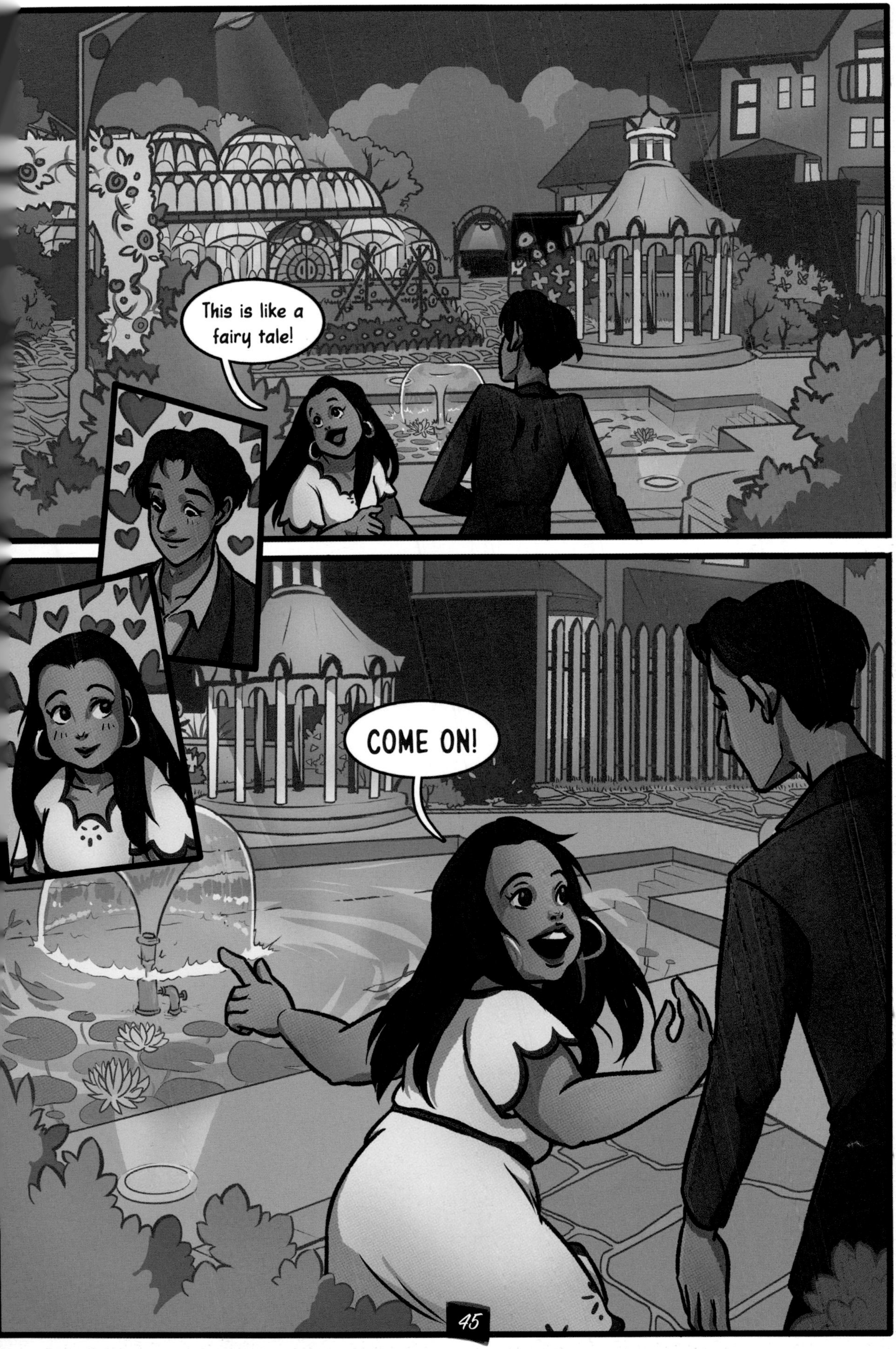
This is like a fairy tale!
COME ON!

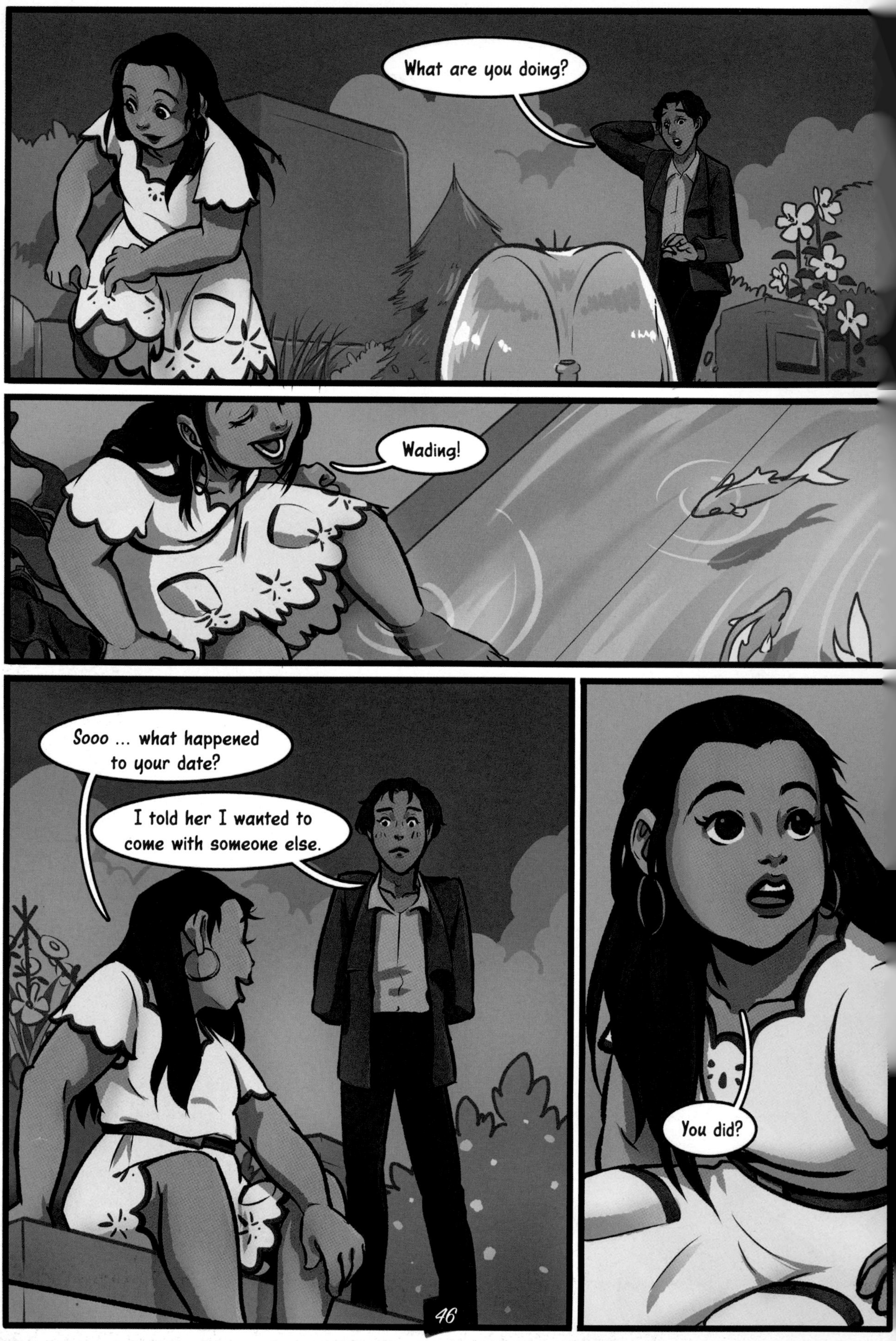
What are you doing?
Wading!
Sooo ... what happened to your date?
I told her I wanted to come with someone else.
You did?

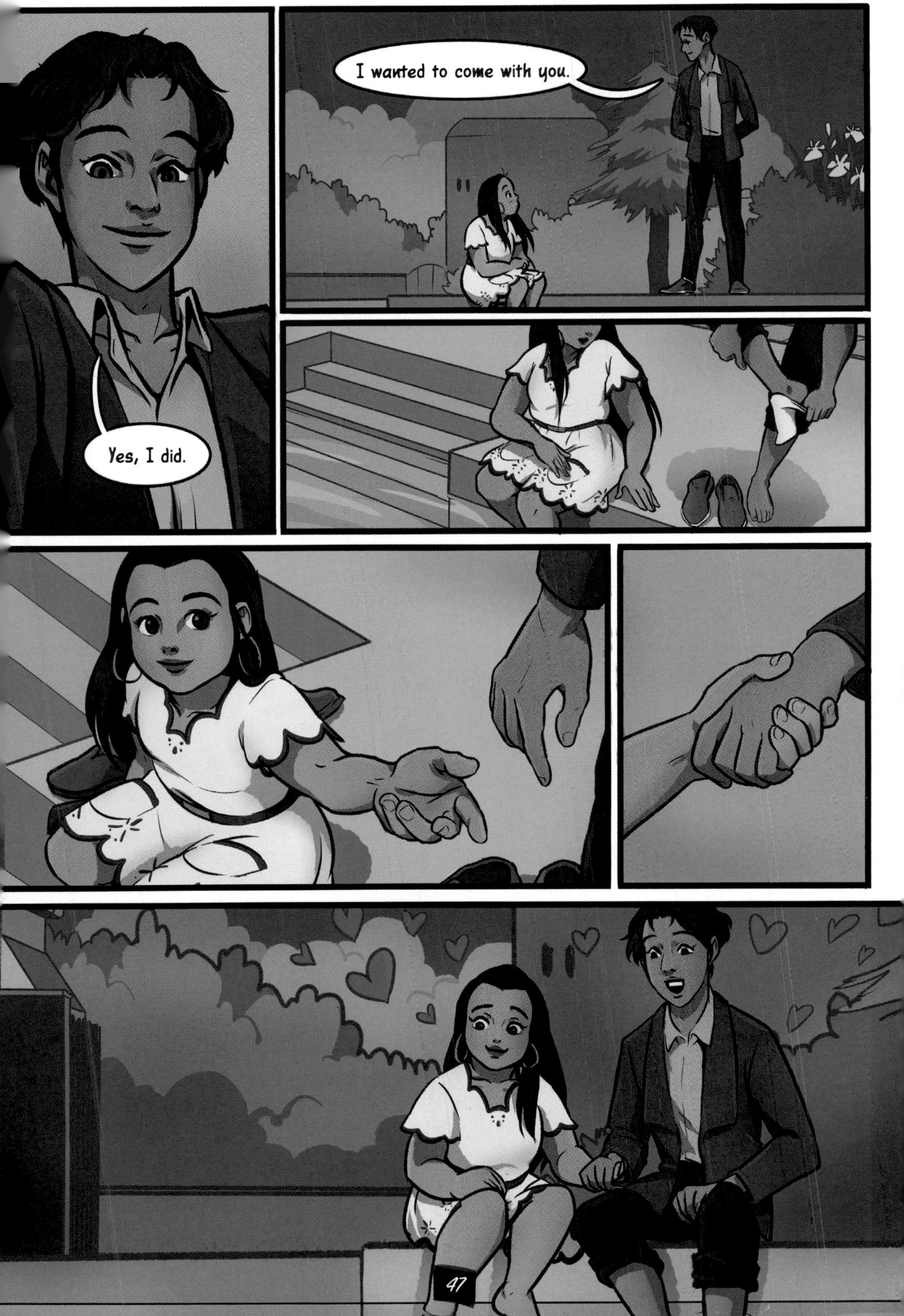
I wanted to come with you.
Yes, I did.

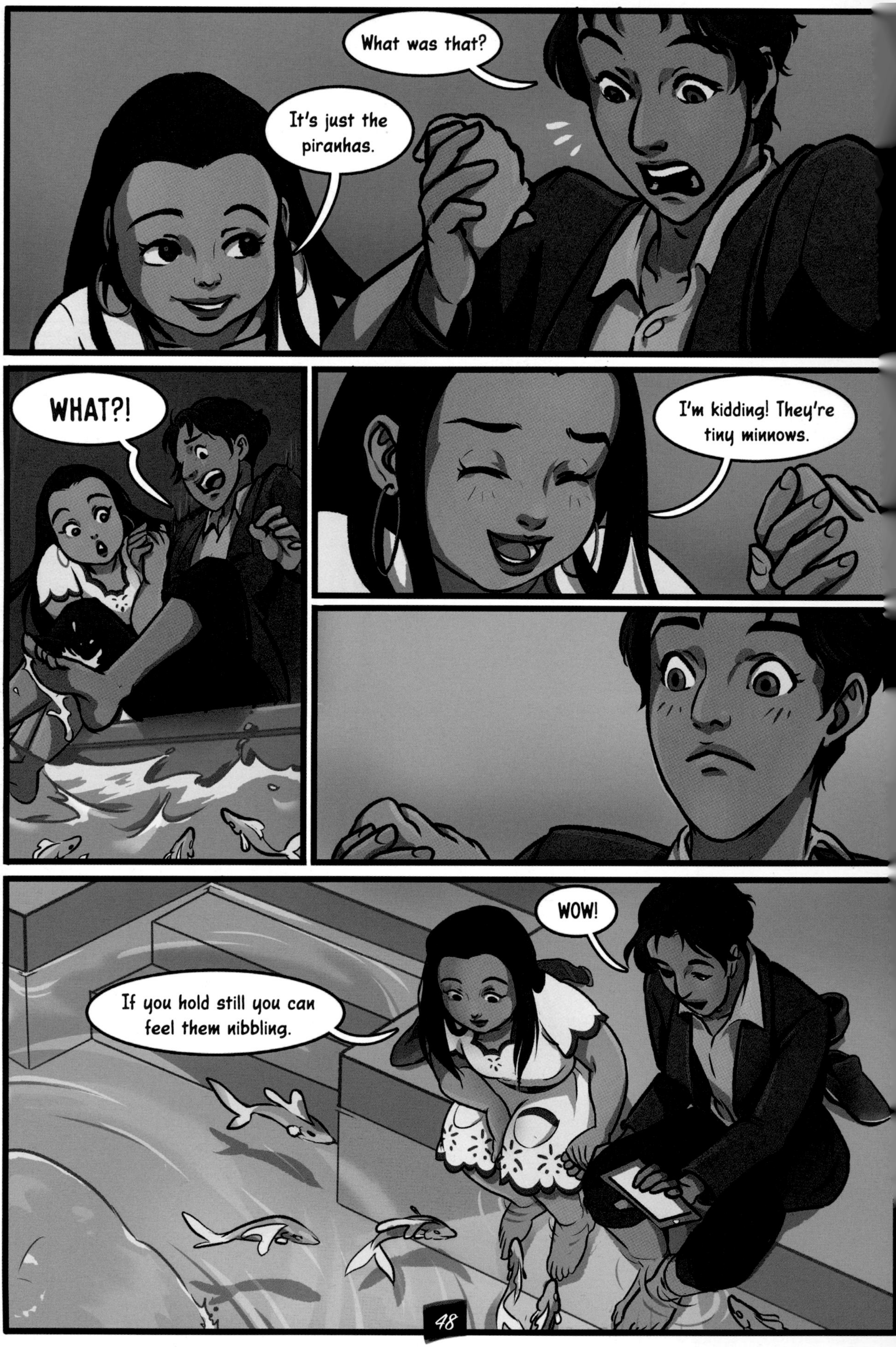
What was that?
It's just the piranhas.
WHAT?!
I'm kidding! They're tiny minnows.
WOW!
If you hold still you can feel them nibbling.

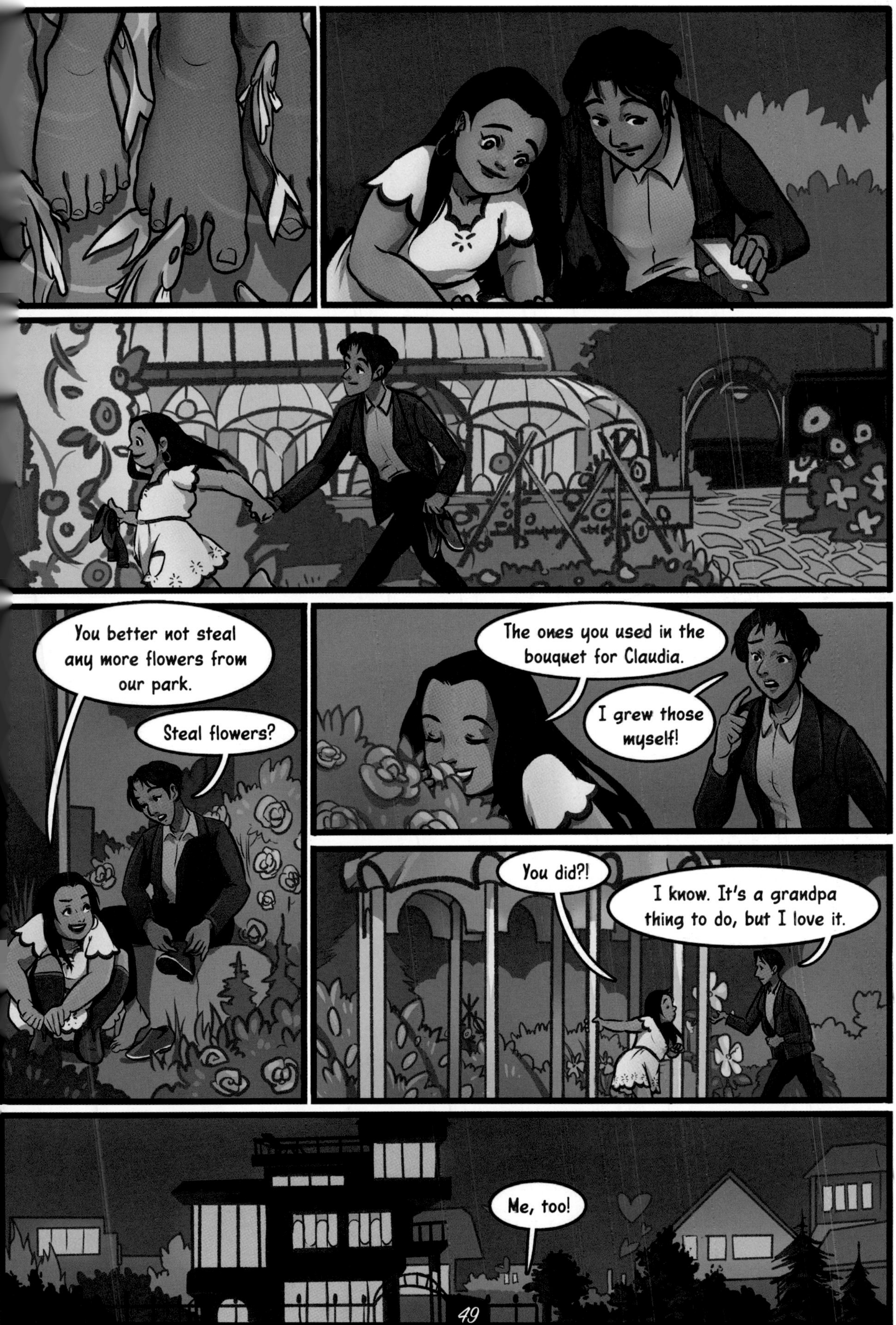
You better not steal any more flowers from our park.
Steal flowers?
The ones you used in the bouquet for Claudia.
I grew those myself!
You did?!
I know. It's a grandpa thing to do, but I love it.
Me, too!

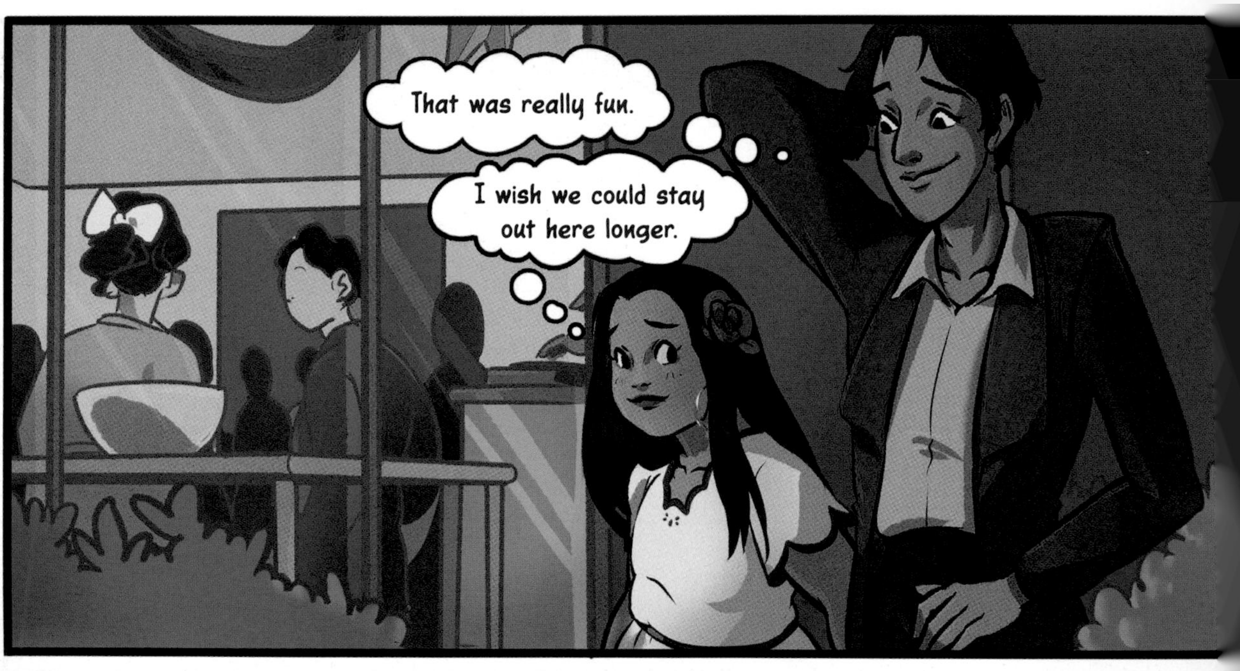
That was really fun.
I wish we could stay out here longer.

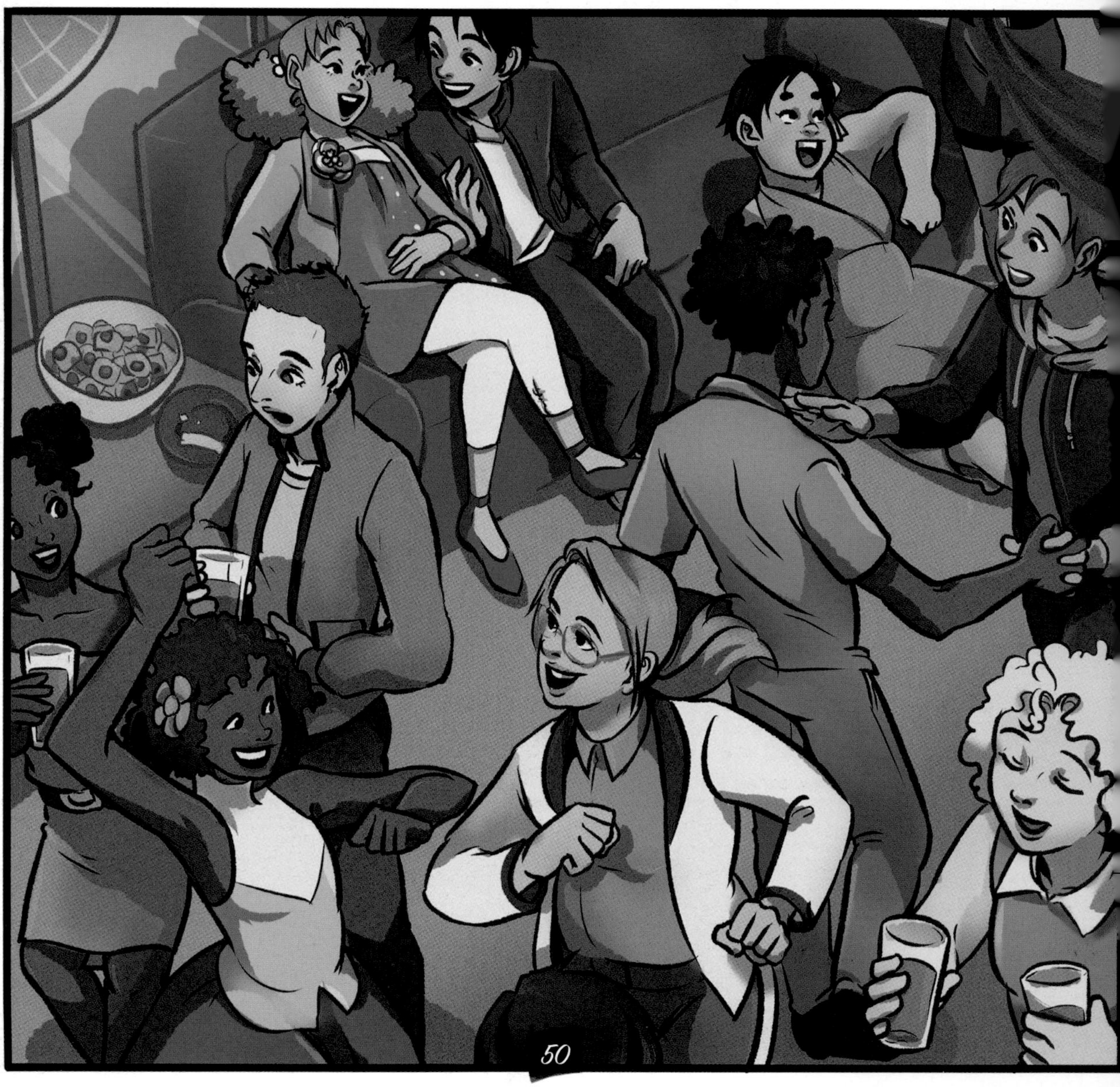

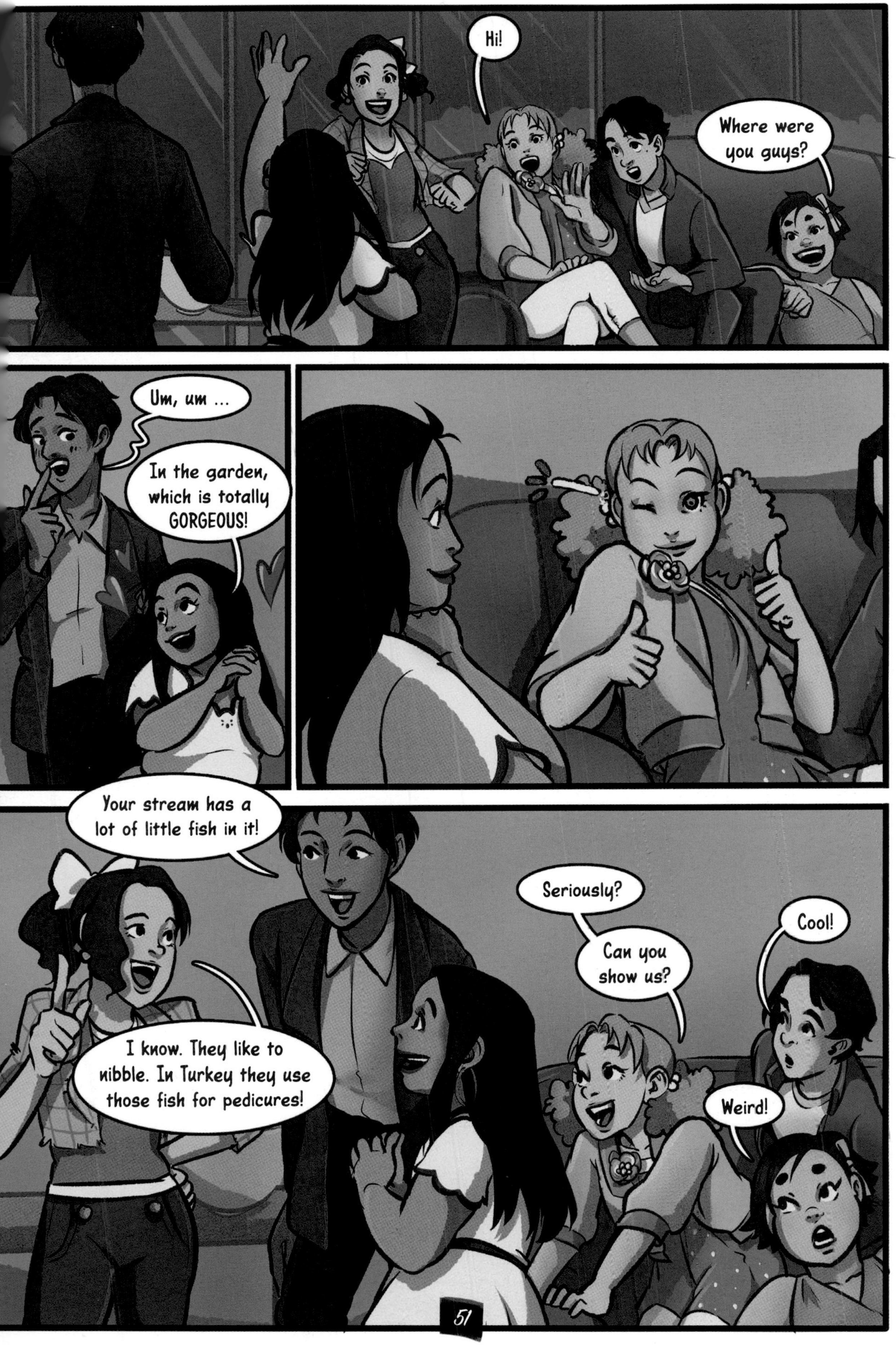
Hi!
Where were you guys?
Um, um ...
In the garden, which is totally GORGEOUS!
Your stream has a lot of little fish in it!
I know. They like to nibble. In Turkey they use those fish for pedicures!
Seriously?
Can you show us?
Cool!
Weird!

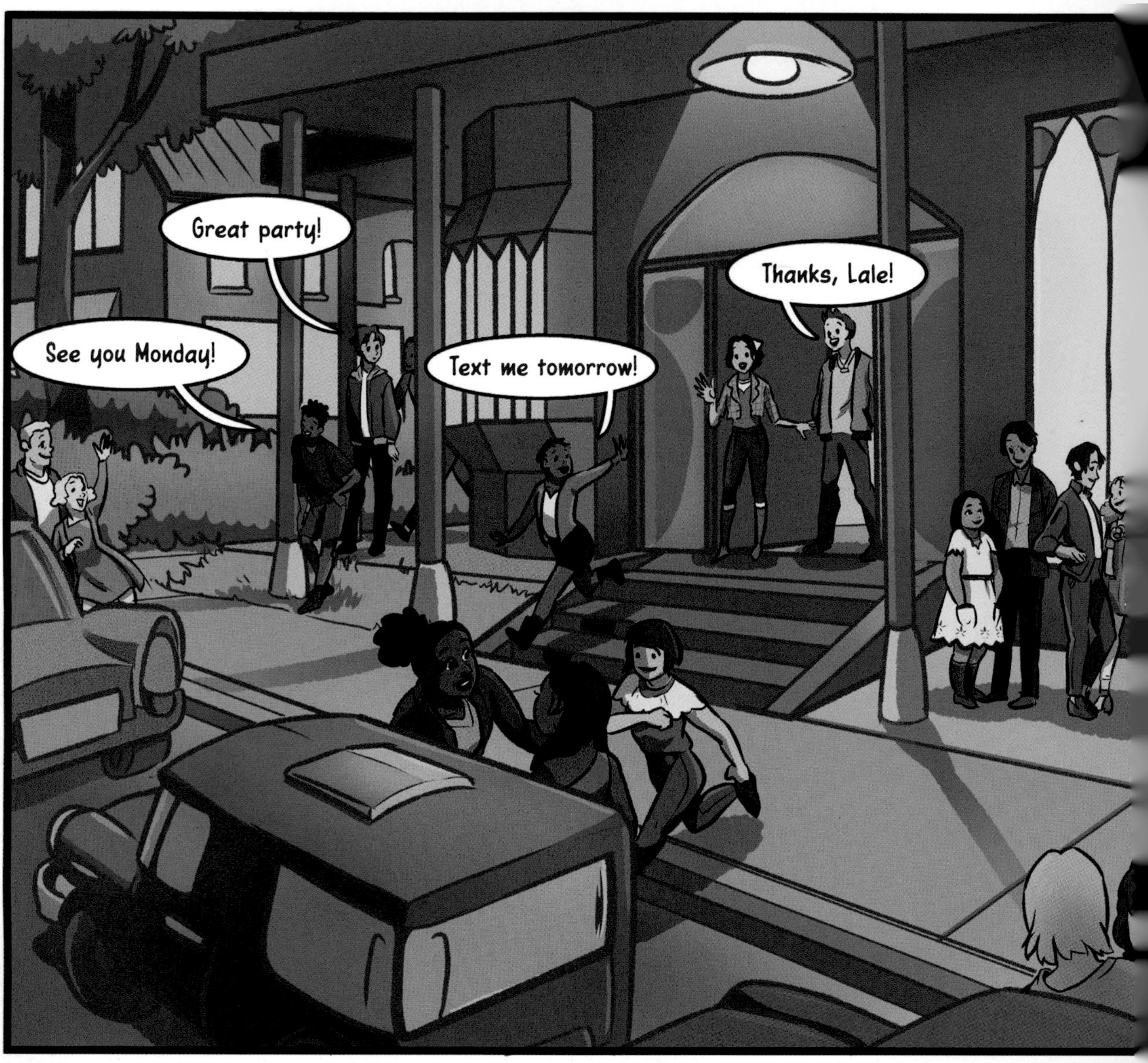
Great party!
See you Monday!
Text me tomorrow!
Thanks, Lale!

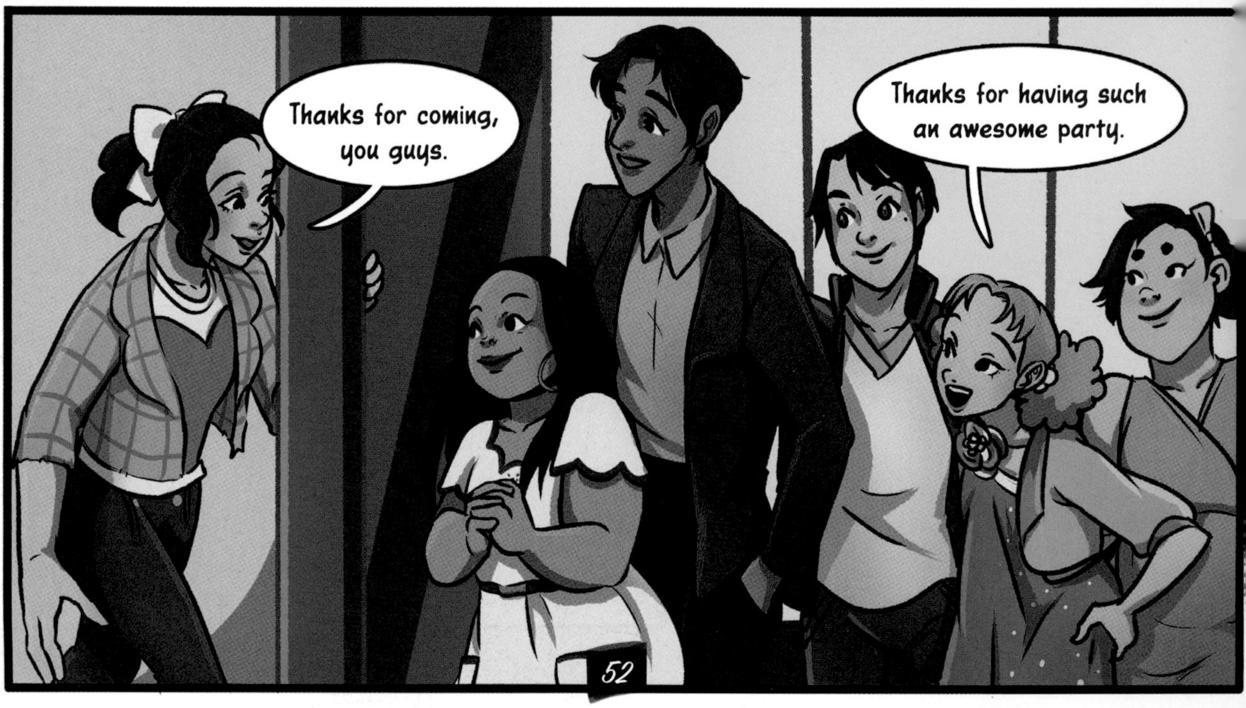
Thanks for coming, you guys.
Thanks for having such an awesome party.

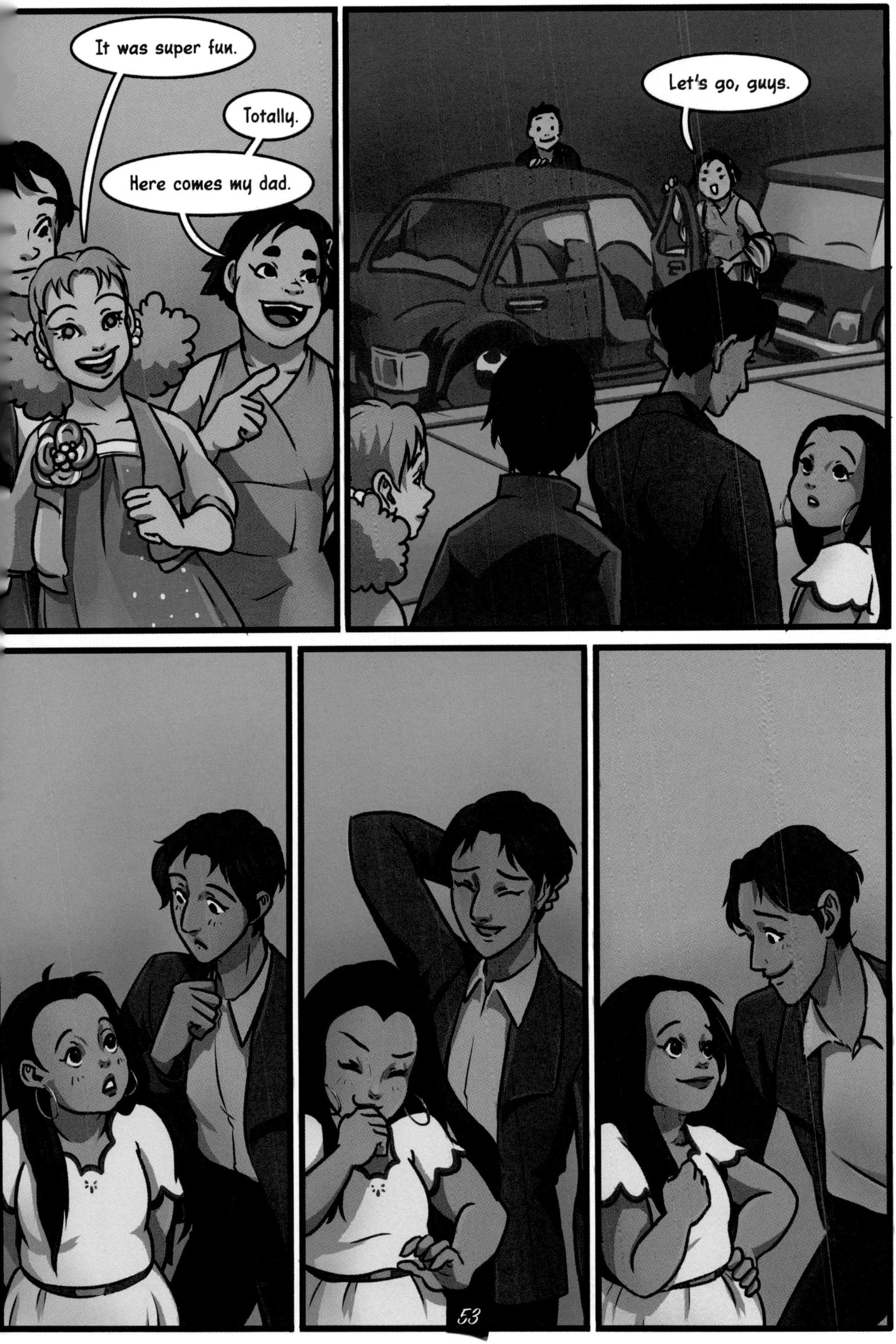
It was super fun.
Totally.
Here comes my dad.
Let's go, guys.

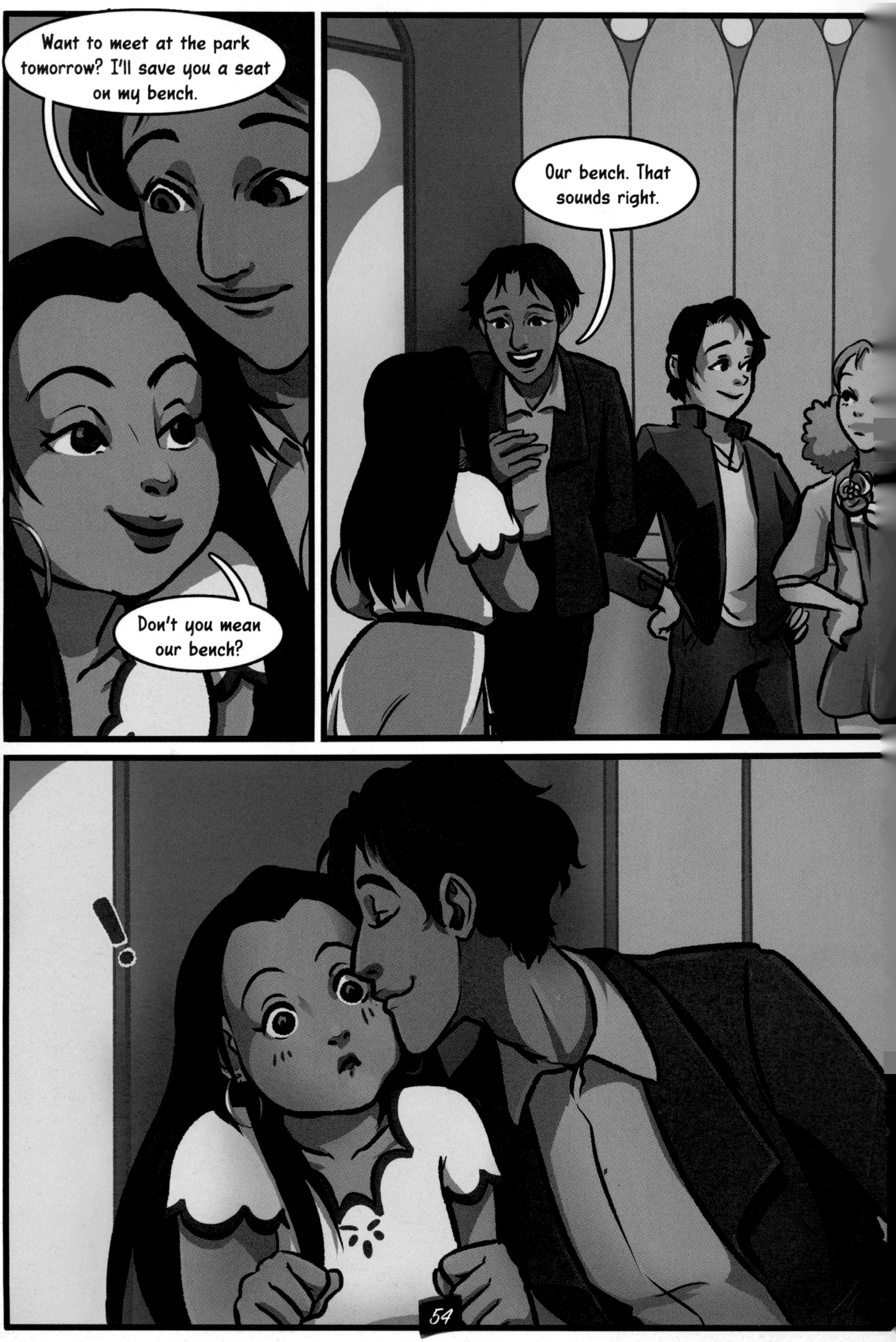
Want to meet at the park tomorrow? I'll save you a seat on my bench.
Don't you mean our bench?
Our bench. That sounds right.
!

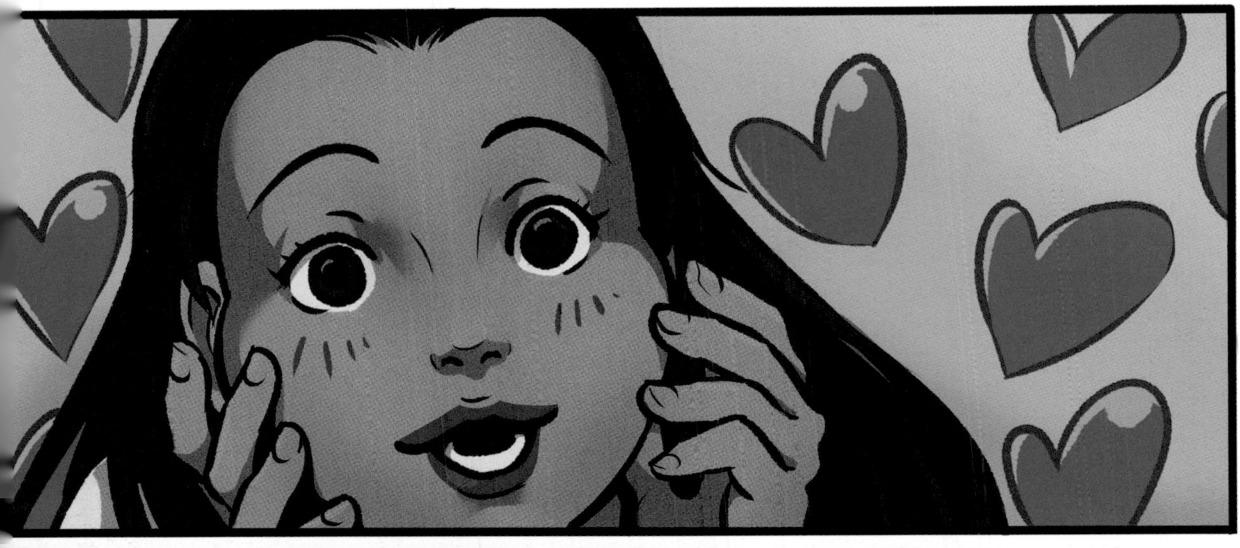

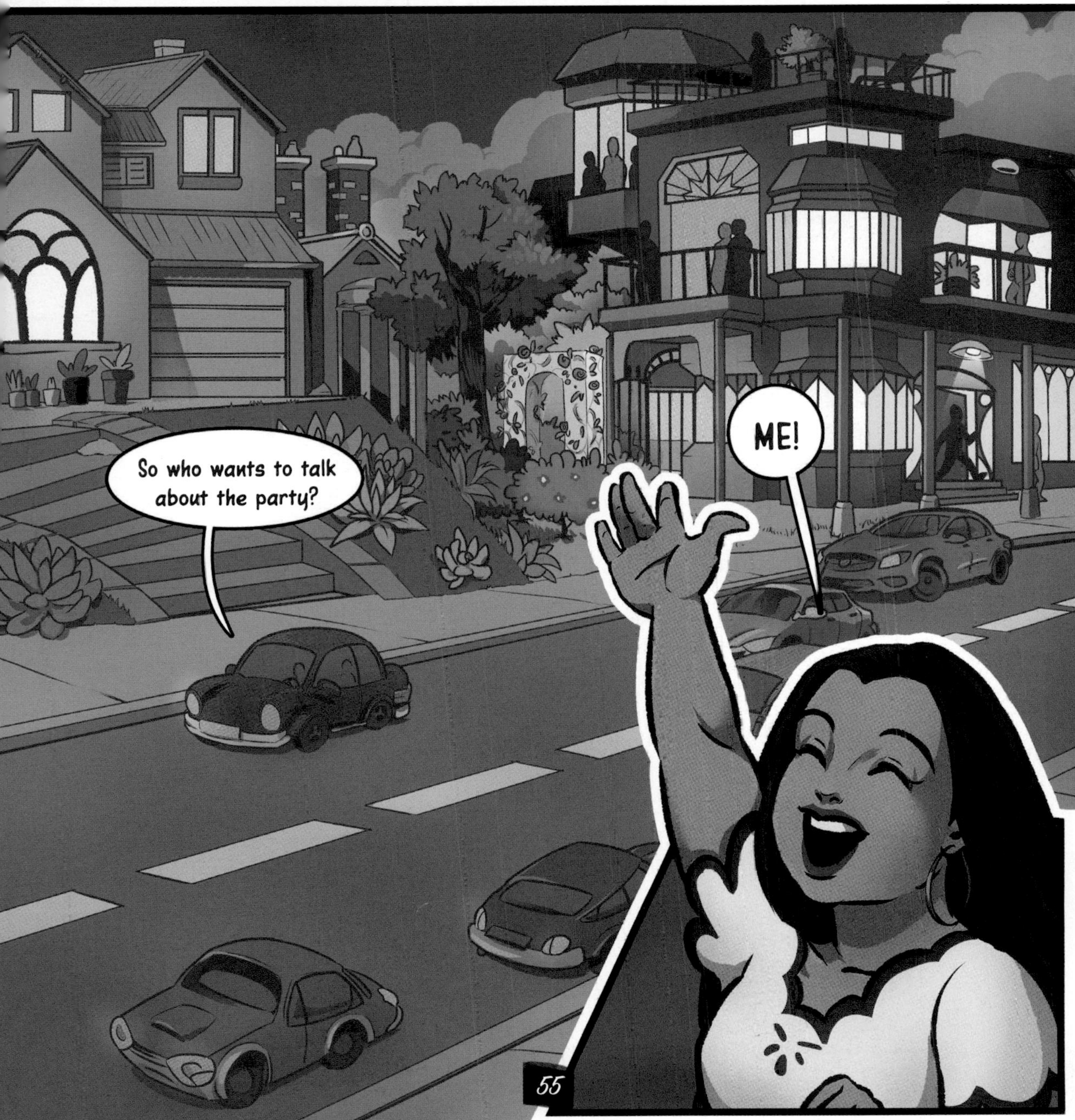
So who wants to talk about the party?
ME!

Gardening for Good

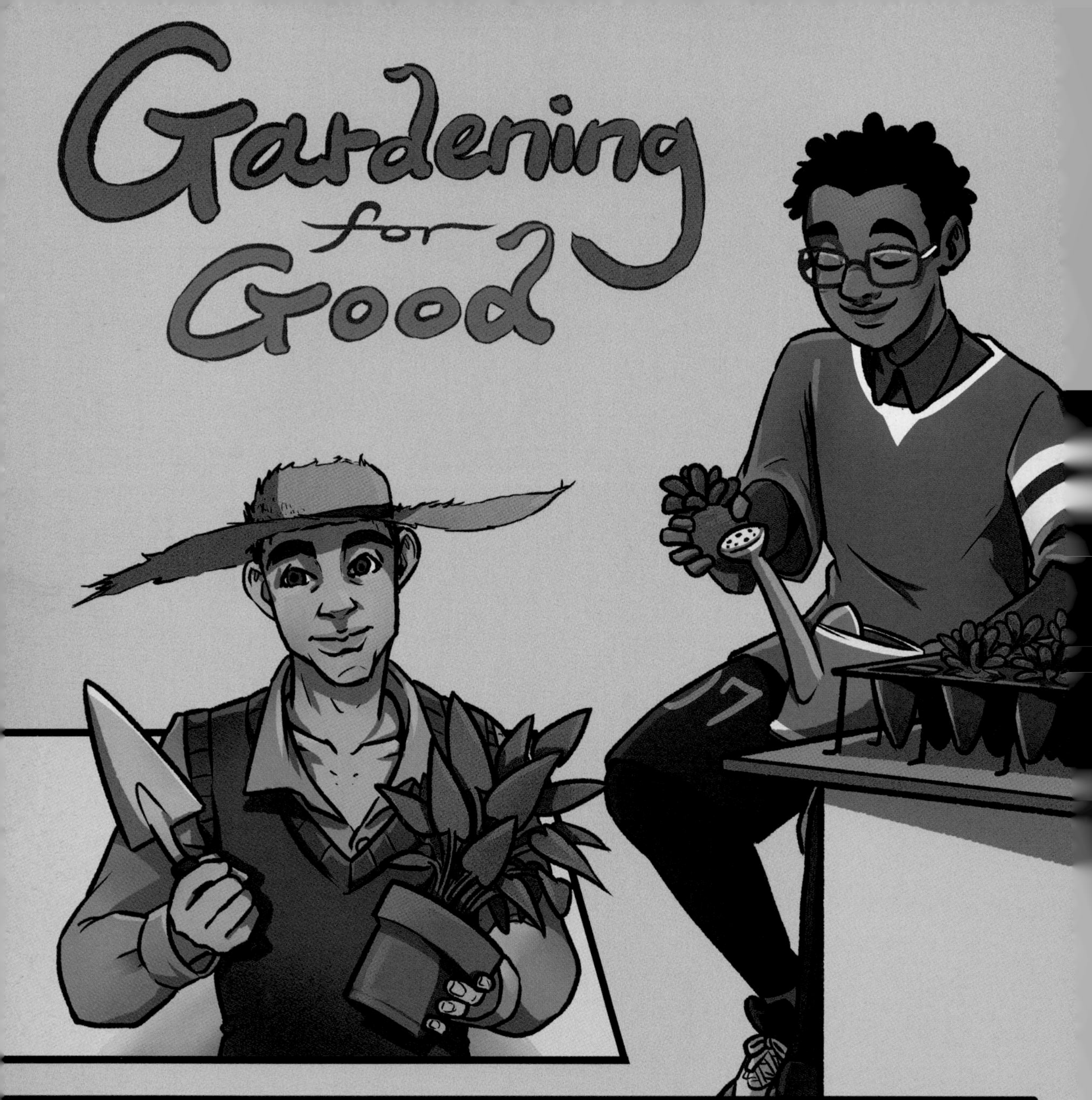

Not only does Mr. Johnson, above left, know a lot about history, he is also a master gardener. Using his green thumb, he helped create an ongoing gardening fund-raiser. Organizations can work with Mr. Johnson to grow and sell plants to earn cash for their clubs.

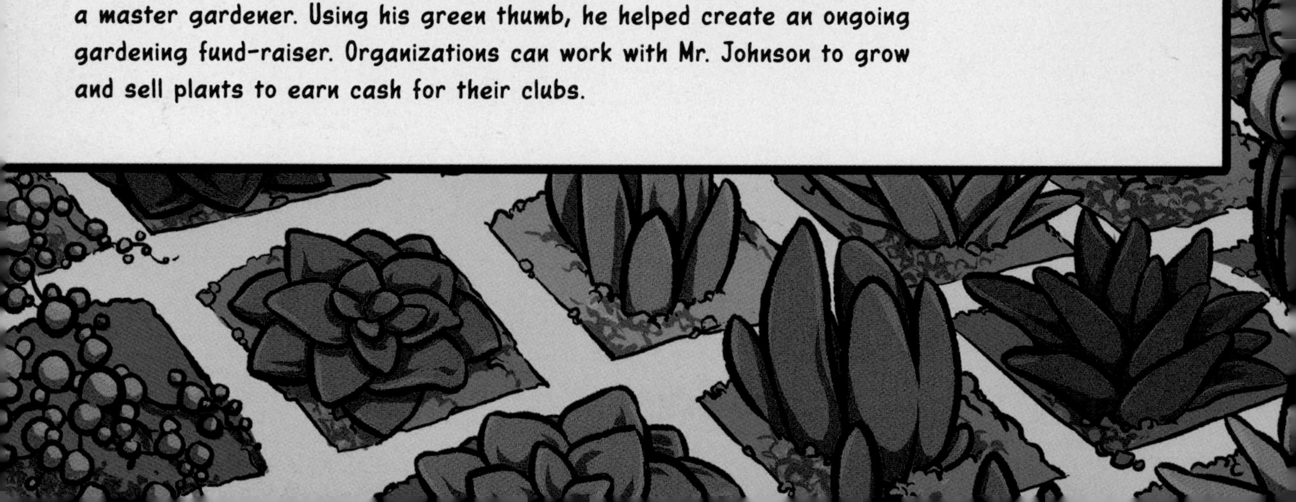

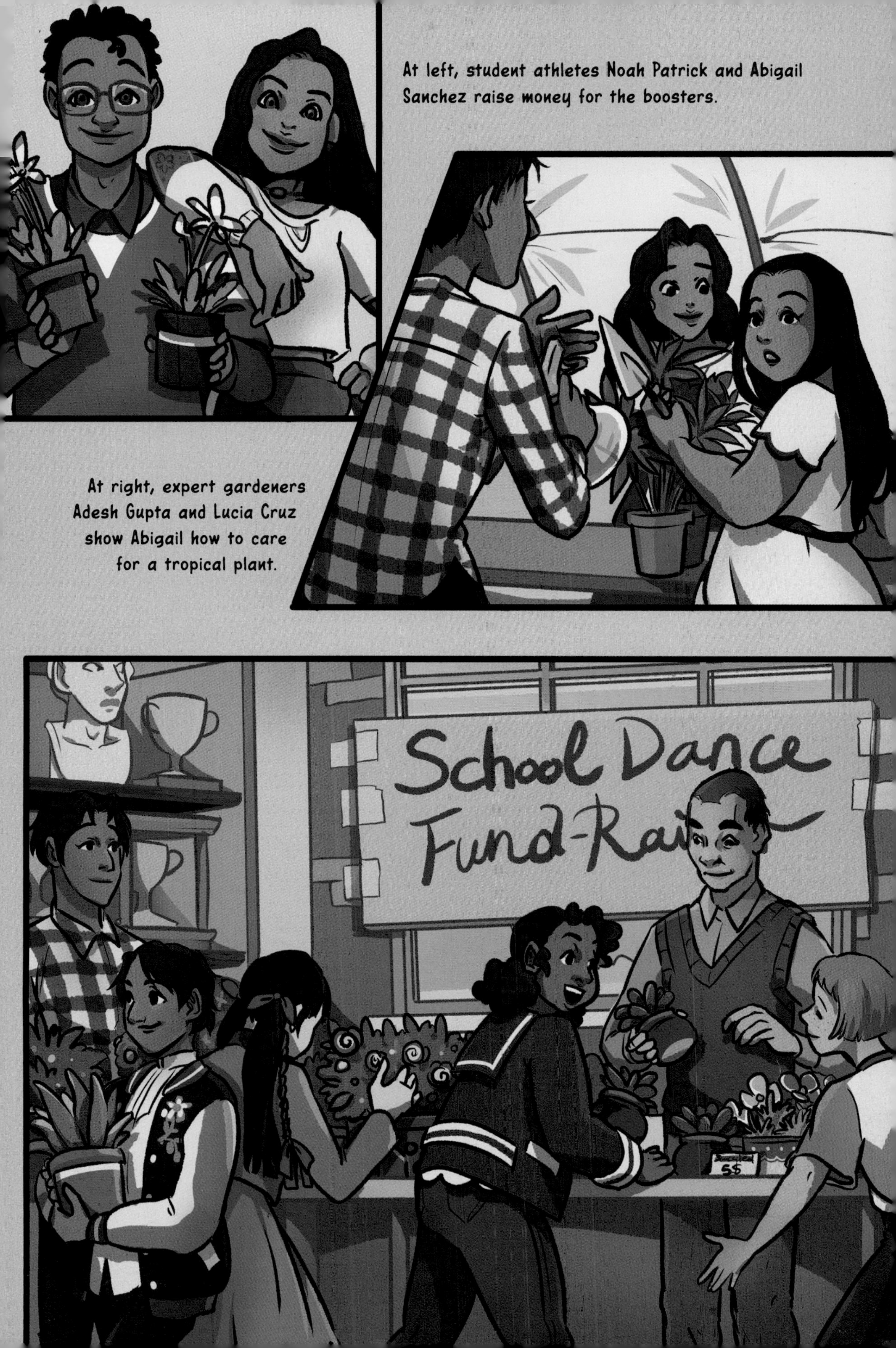
At left, student athletes Noah Patrick and Abigail Sanchez raise money for the boosters.
At right, expert gardeners Adesh Gupta and Lucia Cruz show Abigail how to care for a tropical plant.
School Dance Fund-Rai

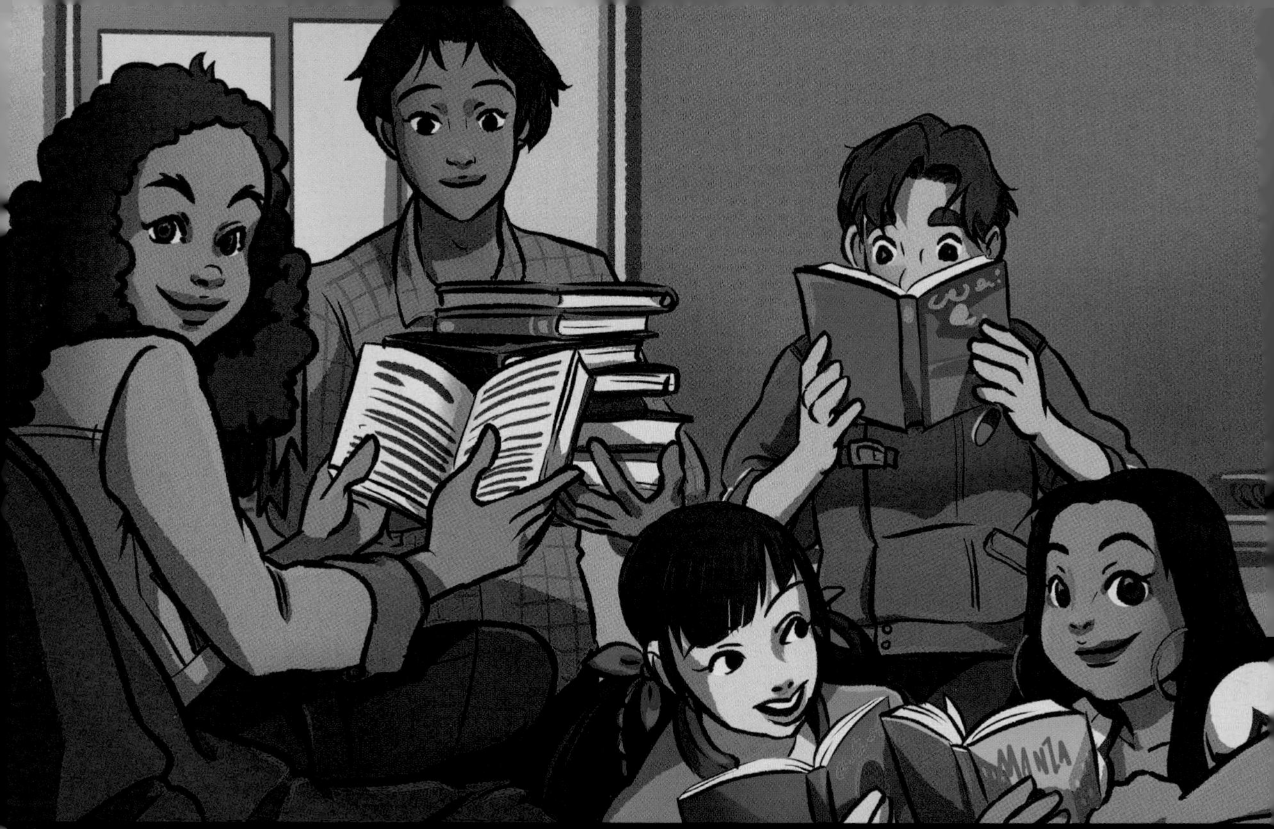

Memorial Book Club

Memorial's biggest readers share their favorite books at a monthly book club. Clockwise from the left: Lilly Rodriguez, Adesh Gupta, Scooter deJesus, Lucia Cruz, and Jasmine Yu.

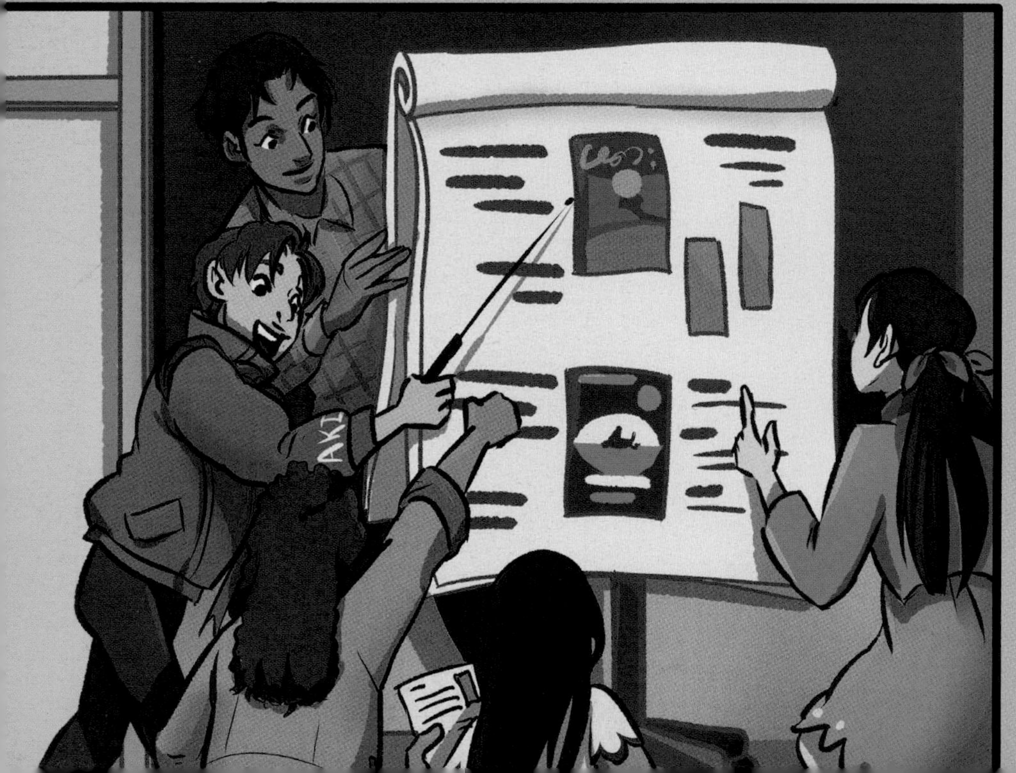
AKI

Each month the club meets to discuss that month's read and choose a new book for the next meeting. At left, members of the club debate the November book choice.

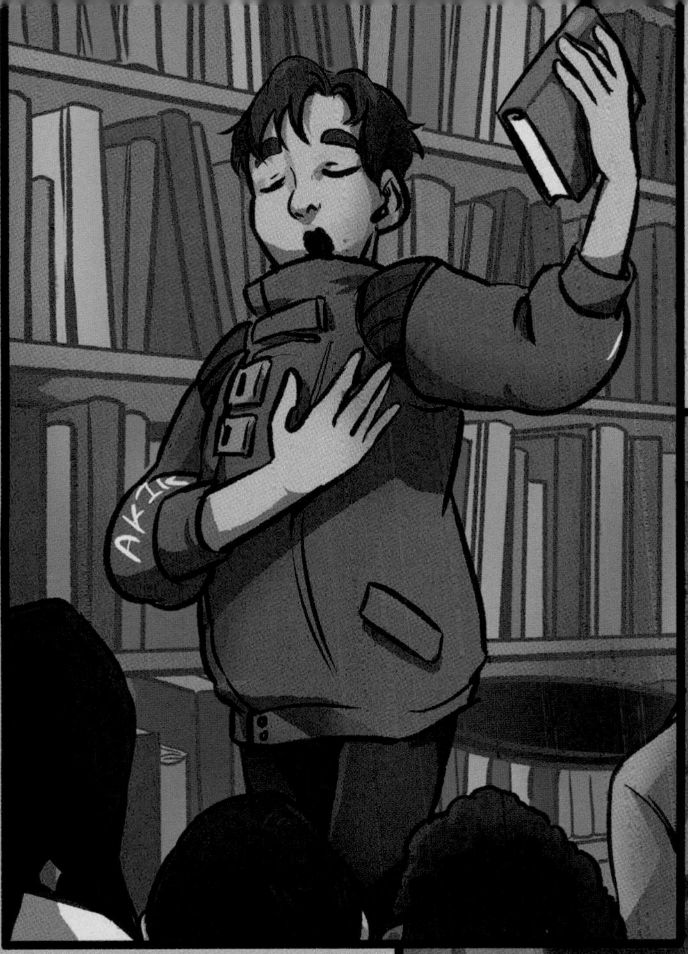

At left, club clown, Scooter deJesus, dramatically recites a passage from December's book, *Railhead* by Philip Reeve.

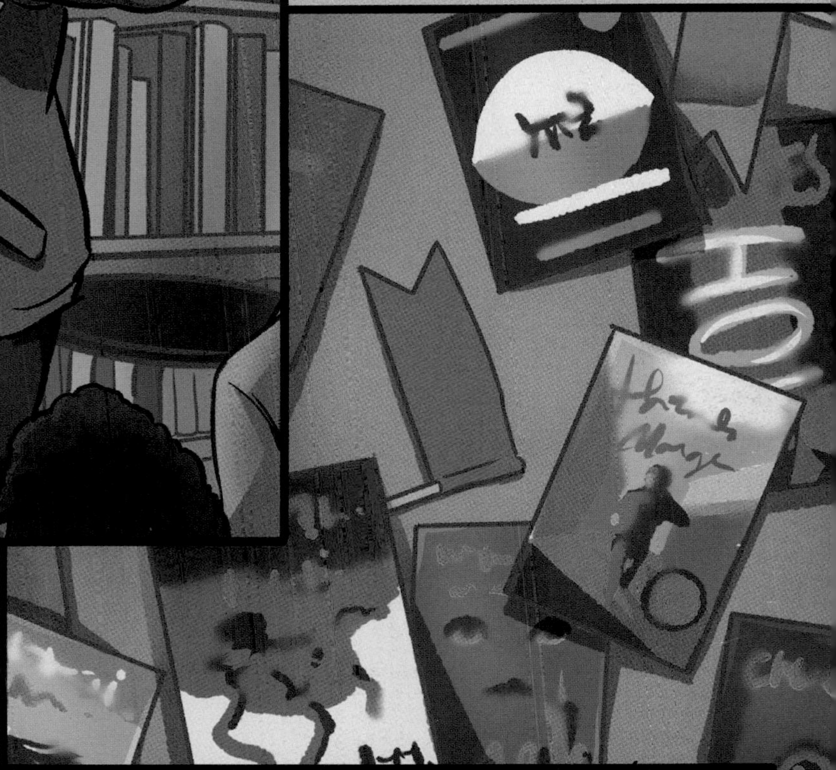

The book club also helps create bulletin boards (at right) for the library.

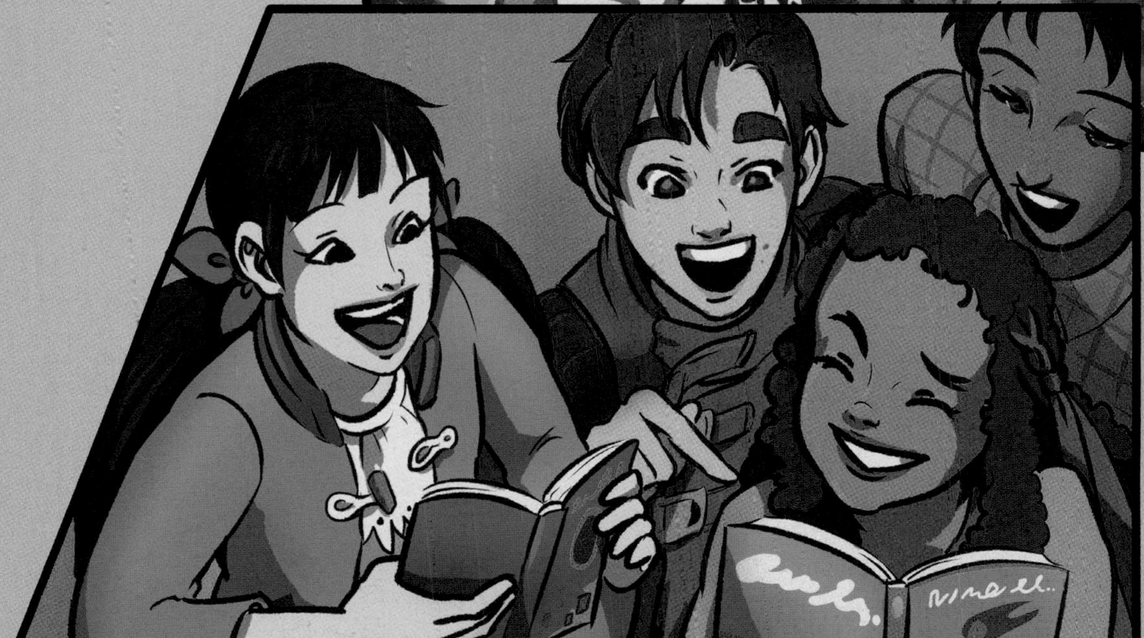

HOLDING HANDS WITH SOMEONE YOU LOVE CAN RELIEVE STRESS.

DATING 101

47% **OF TEENS SHOW THAT THEY LIKE SOMEONE BY COMMENTING, LIKING, OR INTERACTING WITH HIM OR HER ON SOCIAL MEDIA**

56% OF AMERICANS BELIEVE IN LOVE AT FIRST SIGHT

"Continue to share your heart with people even if it has been broken."

—AMY POEHLER

"People aren't defined by their relationship. The whole point is being true to yourself and not losing yourself in relationships, whether romances or friendships."

—NINA DOBREV

AROUND **2/3** OF AMERICANS BELIEVE IN THE IDEA OF **SOUL MATES**

"It sounds like a cliché but I also learnt that you're not going to fall for the right person until you really love yourself and feel good about how you are."

—EMMA WATSON

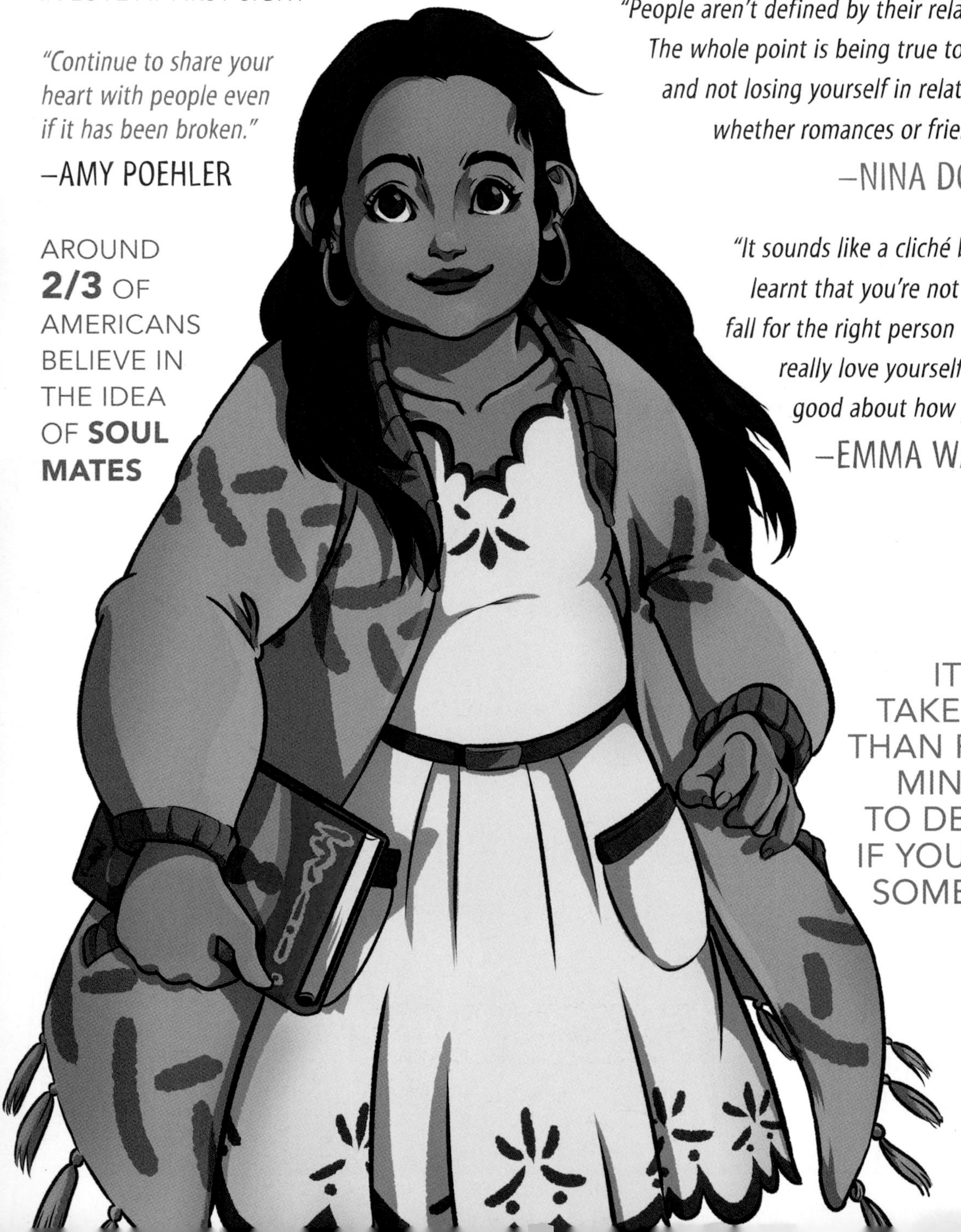

IT CAN TAKE LESS THAN FOUR MINUTES TO DECIDE IF YOU LIKE SOMEONE

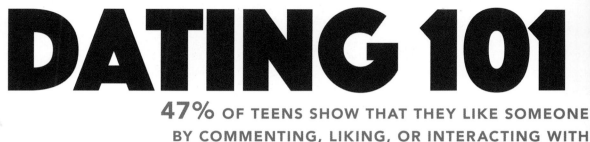

PRE-DATE DRAMA!
A TEXT CHAIN BETWEEN LUCIA AND FLORA

L: HELP. I'm going to the comic book store with Adesh and I am FREAKING OUT.

F: ;) L, you just saw him at Lale's party.

L: But this is our first real date. And there will be people there watching us and what if I don't know what to say and what if it's really, really bad omg.

F: OK. Breathe. It'll be fine. I just had my first date with Josiah, so I am full of wisdom and advice. Let me introduce you to ...

FLORA'S TIPS TO SURVIVING A DATE

1. De-stress. Go for a walk to clear your head. Or jam to some music! Do whatever you can to get rid of your stress so that you're the relaxed, happy Lucia I know you can be.
2. Imagine your date going really, really well. Visualize success, and it'll happen. Trust me.
3. Dress for YOU. Choose clothes that will make you feel great and feel comfortable.
4. Be confident. You are an awesome person. Trust. YOU GOT THIS. Realize and accept that, L.

L: You are so wise.

F: :) obvi. But even I get nervous. Everyone does. I bet you all the comics in your room right now that Adesh is just as nervous as you are.

L: Maybe. I just hope this date goes well. I want him to keep liking me.

F: OK, hang on. I'm going to add Amber to this group. She told me something before my date with J that I think you need to hear.

Amber has been added to this conversation

A: HELLO TO MY TWO FAVORITE GIRLS!

F: Tell Lucia what you told me before my date with Josiah.

A: OMG Flora was a wreck.

L: LOL

F: I was only freaking out a little!!

A: SURE. L, I'm assuming you are also having a heart attack about your upcoming date?

L: Possibly.

A: Well, Adesh is great. But you know, you are too. And your greatness doesn't disappear based on if some boy likes you or not. So go out on that date as the fabulous Lucia we know, and you will rock it!

F: Agree!!

L: Thank you both! :)

GLOSSARY

GORGEOUS – really beautiful or attractive

INESCAPABLE – impossible to avoid

MERENGUE – a style of music and dance that comes from the Dominican Republic

PIRANHA – any of various usually small flesh-eating South American freshwater fishes that have very sharp teeth

REJECT – to refuse to grant or consider

SPANISH TRANSLATION

¿COMO ESTA TU DIA? – How was your day?

FABULOSO – fabulous

¿POR QUE? – why

MI AMOR – my love

MI CLOSET ES TU CLOSET. – My closet is your closet.

QUESTIONS

1. Give three examples of Lucia being a good friend in the story.

2. Imagine that Flora had asked Josiah. How would that have changed the story?

3. Do you think Lucia likes Amber? Use examples from the story to support your answer.

4. How does Lucia's attitude change from the beginning of the story to the end of the story?

CHALLENGE!

Do something nice! Hold the door, help carry a load, or leave a positive message for someone. Even a small gesture can make a big impact.